# URSULA CHANG

# Spring Ruin

ROMANCE

*Copyright © 2025 by Ursula Chang*

*All rights reserved. No part of this publication may be reproduced, stored or transmitted in any form or by any means, electronic, mechanical, photocopying, recording, scanning, or otherwise without written permission from the publisher. It is illegal to copy this book, post it to a website, or distribute it by any other means without permission.*

*This novel is entirely a work of fiction. The names, characters and incidents portrayed in it are the work of the author's imagination. Any resemblance to actual persons, living or dead, events or localities is entirely coincidental.*

*Ursula Chang asserts the moral right to be identified as the author of this work.*

*First edition*

*This book was professionally typeset on Reedsy. Find out more at reedsy.com*

# Contents

| | | |
|---|---|---:|
| 1 | Lila | 1 |
| 2 | Ben | 10 |
| 3 | Lila | 18 |
| 4 | Lila | 24 |
| 5 | Ben | 38 |
| 6 | Lila | 42 |
| 7 | Ben | 53 |
| 8 | Lila | 60 |
| 9 | Lila | 69 |
| 10 | Ben | 77 |
| 11 | Lila | 86 |
| 12 | Lila | 94 |
| 13 | Ben | 102 |
| 14 | Lila | 109 |
| 15 | Lila | 119 |
| 16 | Ben | 132 |
| 17 | Ben | 141 |
| 18 | Ben | 148 |
| 19 | Ben | 162 |
| 20 | Lila | 165 |
| 21 | Ben | 174 |
| 22 | Lila | 184 |
| 23 | Epilogue - Ben | 193 |
| 24 | Thank you! | 203 |

| | |
|---|---:|
| *About the Author* | 205 |
| *Also by Ursula Chang* | 207 |

# 1

# Lila

Email. Check.
Fresh batch of lemon drizzle in the oven. Check.
Crisis management mode? Fully activated.
My fingers fly over the keyboard, typing my third email today—and it's not even 11 a.m. Steam might as well be rising from my head.
"Dear Corporate Robot," I mutter, dripping sarcasm into every word. "Thank you so much for brushing me off again. It's been delightful. Now go and choke on some cake and go away—"
I hover over the **send** button, smirking with satisfaction, then—
**Exhale. Delete.**
I crack my knuckles and start over. I type faster, each keystroke harder than the last. My patience wore thin two days ago, and now it's hanging by a thread.
*Enough with the runaround. I want to speak to the person at the top. No more excuses.*
I finally hit send with more force than necessary and lean

back, glaring at the screen like it might cower in submission. Unlikely.

The development proposal looms in my inbox like a ticking time bomb—a plan to demolish the building that holds **Bloom and Brew**, my mother's beloved florist shop and the cafe I added to keep the business afloat. All to make way for yet another soulless block of luxury apartments.

The thought alone makes my blood boil. Not just because of the countless hours we've poured into this place, but because of what it means to my mother. My mother built it from the ground up thirty years ago when she first emigrated to the UK. It's more than a shop; it's her legacy. When Dad left eight years ago, it became more than just a business—it was the one thing that kept her going, giving her purpose when everything else fell apart. I've fought to keep her dream alive by expanding into a cafe when the flower sales alone weren't enough.

I glance toward the back room, where she's arranging flowers, her face serene and focused, as though the world isn't crumbling around us. She hums softly while trimming a bundle of fresh lilies, completely unfazed.

I can't let her lose it. I won't.

The oven timer dings, snapping me back to reality. I pull out the tray of cakes and inhale deeply, letting the scent of lemon and sugar fill my lungs. Comfort. Stability. It's what Bloom and Brew is built on, and I'll be damned if some corporation takes it away.

My phone buzzes. *Wanker* - aka James Harlow's name flashes on the screen.

Great. Him again.

I debate letting it go to voicemail, but I know exactly what kind of message he'll leave— condescending and wrapped in a fake smile. He's been like this from the start. Dismissive at first, then increasingly short-tempered, like I'm a nuisance he can't quite get rid of. Good, I'll keep pestering until I reach the top.

Bracing myself, I pick up. "Mr Harlow."

"Ms Ng," James says, his tone clipped. "I thought we'd already discussed this. You've raised your concerns. We've taken them under advisement."

"That's funny," I reply, shifting the phone to my other ear, "because from where I'm standing, it looks like you've ignored everything I've requested. No environmental assessment. No public consultation. And judging by your refusal to provide proof, no transparency either."

"We've conducted all the required reviews," he fires back. "The project is compliant with every regulation."

"No proof, no transparency—because there is none," I snap.

He exhales loudly, the sound filled with barely disguised irritation.

"Ms Ng, this project is moving forward with or without your approval. I suggest you focus on adapting to the change rather than fighting it."

My blood boils. "Oh, I'm not fighting it alone anymore, Mr Harlow. I've formed the **Silverbeck Business Coalition**. We're a united front, and we've formally requested a meeting with your development team. We're done being ignored."

"A coalition?" he repeats, his voice dripping with disbelief. "And what exactly do you plan to achieve with this... coalition?"

"Accountability," I reply. "Over a dozen businesses are backing this. We want real answers—not a PR script and we want to hear them from the person who actually calls the shots."

"There's no need to escalate this further." His voice is tight now, his patience wearing thin. "I've already told you—I have the authority to address your concerns."

"Authority, sure," I say, sarcasm dripping from every word. "But we both know you're not the one who makes the real decisions. So how about we skip the middleman and go straight to the top? Who's the actual head of this project?"

There's a pause.

"Ms Ng..." His voice softens, almost patronising. "That won't be necessary."

"I disagree." I push off the counter and pace the cafe. "If you won't set it up, I'll find out who they are myself. Trust me, it won't take long."

His silence stretches.

"You're not going to let this go, are you?" he finally says.

"Nope," I reply, popping the 'p' with extra satisfaction.

He sighs heavily. "Fine. Expect a call soon."

The line goes dead. I set the phone down and take a deep breath, my heart still racing.

"Lila, table four is asking for more oat milk!"

I balance two trays of cappuccinos in my arms, nodding toward Jess. The cafe is packed—students with laptops, couples on coffee dates, and our regulars lounging in the corner as if they've got nowhere else to be.

I thrive on mornings like this, where I'm too busy to think.

"Coming right up," I call back, weaving through tables with practiced ease.

It's past lunchtime when the crowd finally starts to thin, and I get my first real break of the day. I head to the counter and collapse on the stool behind the register, grabbing my phone from under a stack of invoices.

Twenty-two unread emails. Three missed calls. One voicemail. The cafe noise hums around me—cups clinking, chairs scraping—but it all fades into the background when I see the unknown number.

I play the voicemail.

I take a deep breath and bring the phone to my ear.

"Ms Ng, this is Ben Ashcroft."

The name slams into me like a freight train. My breath catches.

It can't be.

*Not him.*

My stomach does a weird little flip at the sound of his voice. It's deep, polished, and calm in a way that demands attention.

"You've been persistent about speaking with someone at the top," he continues. "I thought it was time we connected directly. Call me back at your earliest convenience."

I blink at the phone, playing the message again just to be sure I heard it right. Ben Ashcroft.

No. Absolutely not. That Ben Ashcroft wouldn't be calling me in a suit and tie, sounding like he's got the weight of a multinational corporation resting on his shoulders. He wouldn't be leaving smooth, formal voicemails and calling me **Ms Ng** like we've never met before. *He wouldn't even recognise the name—Ms Ng. That's what I go by now.*

I snort. *Definitely not him.*

It's just a coincidence. A completely different Ben Ashcroft.

Still, my hands aren't entirely steady when I set the phone down. Almost three o'clock. No point in waiting—I need answers, and I need them now.

I take a steadying breath and press the number.

It rings twice before a calm, polished voice answers. "Ashcroft Holdings. How may I direct your call?"

"Hi, I'd like to speak with Ben Ashcroft, please," I say, trying to keep my tone professional.

The woman pauses, and I hear the faint clatter of a keyboard. "May I ask what this is regarding?"

"It's regarding the Silverbeck redevelopment project. I've spoken with James Harlow multiple times, but I insist on speaking to the head of the development directly."

There's a longer pause this time, just enough for me to picture her rolling her eyes and deciding how unimportant I am. "Mr Ashcroft is in meetings all afternoon. I can pass along a message—"

"He's expecting my call," I interrupt, injecting as much authority as I can manage.

Another pause. This one feels deliberate. "Hold, please."

Soft jazz trickles through the line—smooth, meant to calm people like me down. It does the opposite. My foot taps out a quick rhythm on the floor, each note stretching my patience thinner.

Finally, the line clicks.

"Ms Ng." His voice is deep and deliberate, his words slow and measured, as if every syllable is carefully chosen. "I believe you've been asking for me."

That voice. Dark, controlled, commanding.

For a split second, I'm sixteen again, throwing pennies into the water fountain. But that boy didn't have this voice.

I force a steady breath, pushing the memory aside. It's just a coincidence. A different Ben Ashcroft. One with far too much authority and a voice that could cut glass.

"You did say 'at my earliest convenience,' Mr Ashcroft," I reply. "And this is it."

"What can I do for you?"

There's an ease in his tone, like he has all the time in the world to deal with this call. It grates on me.

"I'm sure you're aware that I've been in contact with James Harlow regarding the development," I begin, my voice steady but sharp. "I've made it clear that this project is raising serious concerns for the local businesses affected. The Silverbeck Business Coalition has formally requested a meeting with someone who actually has decision-making power. Someone like you."

"Ah, the coalition," he says, his tone thoughtful. "James mentioned it."

"Then you'll also know we're not going away quietly," I say, pressing my advantage.

He pauses just long enough to make me uncomfortable.

"Persistent," he says finally. "I admire that."

I don't trust the warmth in his voice. It feels like a test, a subtle chess move to see how I'll react.

"Well, persistence pays off," I say. "I assume you're willing to meet with us?"

He hums softly, like he's considering it far more than necessary. "Of course. I'd be happy to meet… next month."

"Next month?" My grip on the phone tightens. "We were aiming for something sooner."

"Unfortunately, my schedule is rather full." His voice stays calm, but the deliberate weight behind his words is impossible to miss. "But… well."

Another beat of silence.

"I do have an opening next Wednesday," he continues, like

he's granting me a favour.

"That should give you and your coalition plenty of time to prepare."

I bite down on my frustration. He's controlling the timeline, holding the cards close to his chest—and he knows it. But I'm not about to give him the satisfaction of rattling me.

"Fine," I say, keeping my tone light. "We'll see you next Wednesday at one. Bloom and Brew cafe."

There's a short pause, like he's considering his next move. "I'll be there. I'm looking forward to hearing your spirited opinions."

"I'm sure you are."

"Until then, Ms Ng." His voice dips slightly on my name— just enough to send an unwanted ripple through me.

The line clicks off, and I lower the phone, breathing through the rush of adrenaline that leaves me slightly unsteady.

That was not how I expected this conversation to go.

The date is set. Time to make sure we're ready for whatever slick corporate spin he tries to throw at us. My hands feel shaky as I place the phone back on the counter.

"Wednesday," I mutter to myself, tapping my fingers on the counter. "Bring your best suit, Mr Ashcroft. This isn't going to be a friendly coffee chat."

In the back room, my mum hums softly again, snapping a stem and tucking it into an arrangement. I walk over, past the rows of neatly trimmed roses and tulips, and watch her work for a moment. She glances up with a warm smile, her eyes crinkling at the corners.

"You're thinking too much," she says.

"How can you tell?"

"Because you always get that little line between your eyebrows when you do."

She studies me for a moment, her gaze soft but searching, then asks, "Was that the developers on the phone?"

I hesitate just a second too long, but nod. "Yeah. I managed to organize a meeting. Next Wednesday."

Her smile falters, and she presses a flower into the arrangement. "Oh," she says quietly. "That's... soon, then."

I can hear the worry in her voice, see it in the way her fingers still against the petals. It twists something deep inside me. She shouldn't have to worry about fighting to keep her own shop standing.

I reach over, squeezing her hand. "Mum, I've got this under control," I say firmly. "I promise."

She nods, but the tension in her shoulders doesn't ease. She tries to hide it, to be strong, but I see the worry in her eyes, the way her fingers hesitate over the flowers she's arranging and that's what hurts the most.

I've been handling things like this for as long as I can remember—translating letters, filling out forms, making calls—because English wasn't my parents' first language. Even as a kid, I was the one making sure nothing slipped through the cracks, the one standing between them and the bureaucratic mess that always seemed stacked against us.

I'll do it again.

If saving **Bloom and Brew** means stepping into the lion's den, I will.

# 2

# Ben

"You're telling me you can't manage a cafe owner?"

I lean back in my chair, arms crossed, watching as James pinches the bridge of his nose like he's seconds from losing his shit. James lets out a short, sarcastic laugh, shaking his head. "Plus she's a florist, Ben. Don't forget that."

James exhales sharply, rolling his neck like he's trying to shake off the irritation. He's been with me since the beginning, back when we were just two broke apprentices in steel-toed boots, laying bricks for someone else's paycheck. We worked on other people's projects, building houses we could never afford, until I decided I was done lining their pockets.

I took the risk—left the security of working for someone else and threw everything I had into my first deal. James didn't hesitate. He was there, just like always, backing me up even when it made no sense. And when it paid off—when the business grew and I needed someone I could trust at my side—there was never a question. It was always James and yet, here he is, looking like a florist has just wrecked his entire week.

"She's persistent. Every time I think I've handled it, she

comes back with something new—an environmental assessment, now a business coalition."

He practically growls the last word.

I smirk. Oh, this is entertaining.

"I've dealt with push back before, but this one? She's got teeth."

I raise a brow. "So, you're telling me a florist is outmanoeuvring you?"

James scoffs. "Oh, fuck off. It's not just her. She's got backup. The business owners, hell, I wouldn't be surprised if she starts chaining herself to the building next."

I chuckle. Now that I'd pay to see.

"She's demanding a meeting," he grinds out. "With you."

"With me."

"What, London too comfortable for you now? You forget how to handle business in the trenches?"

I shoot him a dry look. "That's what happens when you're the boss."

"She wants to deal with the head honcho." He tilts his head, eyes glinting with something close to amusement. "Don't you come from Nottingham? You could throw in a family visit with it at the same time."

I keep my expression blank, but my grip tightens on the desk. It's been years. And I like it that way. I push back from my desk, standing to my full height. "Fine. I'll handle it."

James smirks, cocky as ever, like he's just passed off a particularly irritating problem. "You do that and when you realize what a stubborn pain in the ass she is, I'll be here. Waiting. Laughing."

As I pass, I clap a hand on his shoulder, squeezing just enough to be a dick about it. "James?"

"What?" He glares, already knowing I'm about to wind him up.

I smirk. "Next time, try not to get outplayed by a florist."

His scoff follows me down the hall. "Fuck all the way off, Ashcroft."

Real decision-making power. My lips curve into a slow, humourless smile. That's what she wants, is it?

The line rings. Once. Twice. Three times.

Just as I'm about to hang up, the voicemail kicks in.

"This is Lila Ng. Leave a message, and I'll get back to you as soon as I can."

Her voice is smooth, calm, with just the faintest husky edge. Confident. Collected. A little too controlled. It's the kind of voice that lingers in the back of your mind, refusing to be ignored.

Something about it snags my attention, but I can't quite place why.

Ng. The name doesn't ring any bells, but her voice... It feels familiar, like a song I've heard before but can't remember the lyrics to.

I hesitate, my thumb hovering over the end-call button. I could hang up, let her wonder. That would be the smart move — keep her waiting.

But then I change my mind.

"Ms Ng," I say, my voice low and deliberate. "This is Ben Ashcroft."

I pause for effect, measuring my words carefully.

"You've been persistent about speaking with someone at

the top," I continue, my tone smooth but firm. "I thought it was time we connected directly. Call me back at your earliest convenience."

I end the call and sit back in my chair, drumming my fingers on the desk. Something tells me this isn't going to be a typical meeting.

I lean back, staring at the ceiling. I'll wait for her callback.

An hour passes. Then three.

I glance at my phone, the number I called earlier still in my recent calls. Nothing.

A slow burn of irritation creeps up my spine. Most people scramble to return my calls immediately, bending over backward to accommodate my schedule. But not Ms Ng.

The fact that she's not playing by the usual rules only makes me more curious—and more annoyed.

I've moved on to reviewing another report when the phone rings.

"Mr Ashcroft, there's a Lila Ng on the line."

I set my pen down slowly, masking my irritation behind a calm exterior. Hours later. She's calling hours later.

"Put her through," I say, my voice calm, measured.

Claire hangs up, leaving me alone with the blinking line. I let it ring once. Twice. Three times.

Make her wait.

Finally, I press the button.

"Ms Ng," I say smoothly, my tone sharper than it was earlier. "I was wondering if you were ever going to call back."

There's a slight pause, barely a beat, before her voice comes through—steady and unaffected.

"You did say 'at my earliest convenience,' Mr Ashcroft," she replies. "This is it."

I smirk, despite myself. Bold. I like that.

"So," I say, bringing us back to business. "What can I do for you?"

She jumps straight in, laying out her argument with precision and efficiency. No unnecessary pleasantries. No hesitation.

Most people plead, try to appeal to the company's goodwill. She doesn't. She's not asking for a meeting. She's demanding one.

Her voice is sharp, controlled, but there's a heat beneath it. Passion. Frustration. Fight.

I listen, more focused on the way she speaks than the words themselves.

She pushes without pushing too hard. She knows exactly when to hold back.

Impressive. Most people don't know how to handle me.

I tell her the meeting will be next month. Let the frustration build. See how she handles resistance.

As expected, she pushes back immediately.

"Next month?" Her voice sharpens. "We were aiming for something sooner."

I smirk. Predictable.

I smile, sensing the tension behind her words. She's trying to take control. I respect that—but she's not in charge here. I let the pause stretch just long enough to make her wonder if she's overstepped. Make her feel the weight of silence.

Then I exhale, as if I'm making an exception.

"Unfortunately, my schedule is full." I keep my tone smooth, impassive. "But... well. I do have an opening next Wednesday."

Another pause. I imagine her grinding her teeth, hating that I've dictated the terms.

"Fine," she says lightly, but there's an edge beneath it. She doesn't like being backed into a corner.

Good.

"We'll see you Wednesday at one. Bloom and Brew."

The cafe. Her turf.

I hum in acknowledgment. "I'm looking forward to hearing your spirited opinions."

"I'm sure you are."

The line clicks off.

I set the phone down, my fingers tapping idly against the receiver. That was... unexpected. She didn't flinch, didn't scramble to appease me like most people do. She pushed back. Matched me.

Curious.

I lean back, considering for a moment before pulling my laptop closer. Let's see what I'm dealing with. I type Bloom and Brew into the search bar. The first image that pops up is of the shop front—covered in flowers, charming but otherwise unremarkable.

Then I see her picture.

Lila.

My breath catches, my pulse steady but heavy. I click on the image, leaning closer.

Sharp cheekbones, full lips, same fire in her eyes. My stomach drops. It's her. Lila. The last person I ever expected to see again. The girl I walked away from. She's standing outside the cafe, one hand resting on her mum's shoulder, a small smile softening her face.

Confident. Effortless. Unmistakably her.

She's laughing—carefree, like the years between us never existed. My chest tightens.

I sit back in my chair, staring at the screen. For a moment, everything else disappears. The reports on my desk, the endless calls and meetings—none of it matters.

Memories hit me like a sucker punch. Her laugh, the way her eyes lit up when she argued with me, the way she tilted her head just before she said something she knew would piss me off.

The way I walked away without a word.

I close my laptop slowly, my heart thudding in my chest.

*What the hell are you doing here, Lila?*

Of all the people who could've stood in my way, it had to be her.

I stand and walk to the window, the London skyline stretching out beneath me—glass towers glinting in the afternoon light, the pulse of power in every direction. My city. My empire.

It's been years since I left Nottingham. I've built a life here in London—clean, controlled, and miles away from the mess I left behind. Far away from her. There's nothing there for me anymore. At least, that's what I thought.

But fate clearly has other plans.

Fifteen years of building my empire, climbing higher with every move. Power, wealth, control—everything carefully crafted. Unshakable. Untouchable.

Does she know who I am? Does she remember?

The way she spoke to me—sharp, confident, like she had nothing to lose—tells me she has no idea who she was talking to.

Not yet.

I grimace, turning away from the window, shoving down the unease creeping through my chest. The thought of stepping back into Nottingham leaves a bitter taste in my mouth. I never planned to set foot there again.

But this is business.

I roll my shoulders, exhaling slowly, grounding myself in logic. Lila Lau is gone. The name that once sat on my tongue so easily, the girl I once—

I cut off the thought before it goes too far.

Ng. A different name. A married name.

Of course she's married. Women like her don't stay single forever.

I open my laptop again, my jaw tightening as my gaze lingers on the photo. Her smile is softer than I remember, her posture still carrying that effortless confidence. She's settled. Happy. Probably has a husband, maybe even kids.

Good. That's good. It means whatever happened between us—whatever she thought we were—it's long buried.

I force my expression neutral. This changes nothing.

Clean cut. Go in, get what I need, and get out. Just like I've always done.

No attachments. No lingering. No second-guessing.

It's worked for years.

It'll work now.

# 3

## Lila

I tap my fingers on the counter, my laptop glowing in front of me. The search bar on the screen mocks me with its uselessness.

*Ben Ashcroft.* Nothing. No LinkedIn. No social media. Not even an outdated company profile.

How is it possible for someone to be this off the grid?

I try again, typing his name with the company name added, hoping it'll spit out more than the generic company website. It doesn't.

"Who doesn't exist online these days?" I mutter, slamming the laptop shut.

"You'll have to wing it," Sophie says, glancing up from her coffee. She's perched on a stool at the cafe counter, watching me with mild amusement. "Mysterious billionaire types are always trouble. You know that."

"This isn't a book," I remind her.

"Could've fooled me," Olivia adds, grinning. "You've got all the elements: the brooding businessman, the small-town girl trying to take him down, a dramatic showdown coming up. Classic enemies-to-lovers vibes."

I roll my eyes, but my stomach twists just thinking about it. "This isn't enemies-to-lovers. This is business. Ben Ashcroft is probably some sixty-year-old fat, balding guy who barely knows how to use email."

Sophie bursts out laughing. "That's the spirit!"

"Uh-huh," Olivia says, raising an eyebrow. "And you've spent the last hour trying to figure out everything about him because...?"

"Because I want to be prepared," I snap, turning back to the engagement flowers. "I'm not walking into that meeting blind."

I snip another stem, trying to focus on the bouquet, but my thoughts keep circling back to that name. I shouldn't care who he is—or if there's even the slightest chance it could be *him*.

But my gut won't let it go.

I glance at my friends, who are deep in conversation, passionately debating the next book for *Books That Bang*—the romance book club Sophie set up. It's been amazing to finally find real people who love romance and smutty books as much as I do. Life has been too busy to find love myself, but books? Books are simpler. No mess, no complications, just guaranteed happily-ever-afters.

*I could tell them.*

I could tell them there's a possibility Ben Ashcroft isn't just some random CEO—that he might be *the* Ben. The boy I never thought I'd see again.

But the words stick in my throat.

Flowers spill across the worktable in the back room—roses, baby's breath, eucalyptus branches—surrounding me like a floral war zone.

The laptop sits next to my notepad, a mess of notes and

printed articles scattered around it.

Olivia scans the paperwork, a pen tapping rhythmically against the table, her eyes narrowing at the chaos around us.

"How can you work like this?" she says, gesturing to the sea of stems, petals, and papers. "There's no order. No system. I'm getting hives just looking at it."

I laugh softly. "Welcome to my brain."

"Seriously, Lila. You've got spreadsheets next to roses, and there's eucalyptus on top of your meeting notes." She shakes her head, muttering to herself. "This is chaos. I can't work in chaos."

"This is creative chaos," I reply with a grin. "It's where the magic happens."

Olivia raises an eyebrow, unimpressed. "Magic or not, it's a miracle you haven't accidentally stapled a flower to your evidence." She slides a stack of papers away from a stray sprig of baby's breath, neatly aligning them.

"See? You're already organising it for me," I tease.

"Someone has to," she says with a sigh. "You're one misstep away from building a bouquet out of legal documents."

I laugh again, the tension easing just a little. Olivia's control-freak tendencies can be maddening, but right now, it's exactly what I need. Olivia scans the paperwork again, her expression softening.

"You're ready," she says, scribbling something in the margin of my notes. "Facts are solid. Structure's good. You've got this, Lila."

I nod, but my stomach still twists. "Thanks. You'd tell me if it wasn't, right?"

"I would." Olivia grins. "This is corporate strategy 101. Trust me, you're ready to make your case."

"But this isn't some company report," I mutter, grabbing a sheet of paper. "This is our home, my mum's business. There's no Plan B if this goes wrong."

Olivia places a steadying hand on my arm. "That's why you'll nail this. Just stick to your facts and control the conversation. Don't let him push you off balance."

I take a breath, exhale slowly, and give her a small nod.

"This meeting feels like the calm before the storm," I mutter.

"Then bring the storm," Sophie says. "Hit him with facts and charm. You're good at that."

"If that fails, seduce him," Willow jokes.

"Not. Helping," I deadpan.

---

I stare at my closet, hands on my hips, chewing on my bottom lip.

Professional but approachable. Not too casual. Not too formal.

Why does nothing feel right?

I grab a navy blouse and hold it up, frowning. Too stiff. Too buttoned-up. The green wrap dress? Too much like I'm trying to make an impression.

I pause, eyeing a pair of tailored black trousers and my favourite fitted blazer—the one that makes me feel like I could walk into a courtroom and destroy someone's life with a well-timed objection. Corporate bitch motherfucker mode activated.

I pull the blazer off the hanger and pair it with a silky black camisole—just enough edge without crossing into cocktail-hour territory. Sleek. Confident. Powerful.

I slip on the trousers and smooth the fabric down, then stand in front of the mirror, tilting my head as I take in the reflection.

Fierce. But polished.

Exactly the energy I need.

I reach for a pair of sharp-heeled black ankle boots and zip them up, the slight clink of the zipper sending a surge of confidence through me. The kind of outfit that makes it clear I'm not to be messed with.

I reach for my jewellery next—simple gold earrings, no necklace—and pull my hair into a low, sleek ponytail. Clean. Powerful. Efficient.

Then it hits me, creeping into my mind without permission. *What if it is him?*

My stomach twists, and my fingers grip the edge of the dresser. No. Stop it, Lila. You're not dressing for him.

I scold myself silently, shaking off the thought. This isn't about him. It never was. This is about protecting the cafe, my mum's shop, and everything we've built.

The armour I've chosen isn't for him. It's for me.

I take one last look in the mirror and square my shoulders. Game on.

The cafe hums quietly around me, the sound of the espresso machine and soft chatter fading into the background as I take my place at the back table.

I stack my notes neatly, adjusting the corners. Everything in order.

For the past hour, I've been watching the clock, the numbers crawling toward 1 p.m. with agonising slowness. I've run through my arguments, rehearsed every possible response, prepared for every counterpoint he might throw at me. This is just another meeting. Another business conversation. Nothing more.

Yet my hands are a little too sweaty. My heartbeat a little too loud in my ears.

I smooth my blazer and lean back in my chair, exuding the kind of confidence I don't quite feel. Fake it until you make it, right?

The door swings open. I don't look up.

Not yet.

But then—something shifts. The air. The energy. A presence.

When I finally glance up—

Oh. My. Fucking. God.

It's him.

# 4

# Lila

Fifteen years later, and he's standing right in front of me, looking like a goddamn magazine cover—taller, sharper, more composed than he ever was at seventeen.

His dark hair is perfectly styled, his tailored suit hugging broad shoulders, not the scrappy, reckless boy I once knew. This man is all muscle, sharp lines and control, his eyes scanning the cafe like he's already decided how the next few minutes will play out.

He hasn't seen me yet.

My pulse pounds. Every instinct tells me to bolt, but I'm frozen.

Then, his eyes lock onto mine. Recognition flashes in his gaze, his lips twitch into something resembling a smile—cool, unreadable, and utterly terrifying.

Shit.

"Ms Ng," he says, his voice lower, smoother than I remember, as he closes the distance between us. His expression doesn't falter, completely composed, like I'm a stranger he's never met before.

He's acting like he doesn't know me.

*What the actual fuck?*

I inhale slowly, swallowing the sharp burn of resentment rising in my throat, and part my lips—ready to greet him, to say something, anything—

But before I can speak, he holds out his hand.

It stops me cold.

Not a smirk. Not a flicker of acknowledgment. Just a calm, detached handshake—like we don't have history.

For a second, I just stare at his hand. It shouldn't matter. It's just a handshake. But something in me hesitates, my fingers twitching at my sides. Do I call him out?

I should leave him hanging. I should cross my arms, tilt my head, let him feel the weight of my silence.

But then—before I can decide otherwise—I take it.

Mistake.

His grip is rough, firm—too familiar. A shiver shoots up my spine before I can stop it. Damn it. His fingers strong around mine, a dozen memories crash into me all at once.

A different time. A different version of him. I force myself to stay still, even though my body is screaming at me to pull away. Break the contact. Stop this reaction.

His thumb brushes against the side of my hand before he lets go, and it takes everything in me not to flinch.

Goddamn it.

I yank my hand back too quickly, heat creeping up my neck. Stupid. That was the stupidest idea. My palm tingles where his skin touched mine, and I curl my fingers into a fist to erase the feeling.

His face remains unreadable, cool and indifferent.

Like he didn't feel a damn thing.

Fine. Two can play that game.

I smooth my expression, meeting his gaze without flinching. "Well, thank you for coming, Mr. Ashcroft." My voice is steady, professional. Almost convincing.

Almost.

His lips curve slightly—not quite a smile, more like he knows exactly what he's doing—and then, smoothly, he says, "Call me Ben."

The words hit like a sucker punch.

I keep my face neutral, but something in my chest tightens. The casual ease of it. Like it's the simplest thing in the world. Like he's still Ben—not the man who disappeared from my life fifteen years ago without a word.

No.

He doesn't get to do that.

I smile—polite, distant, utterly detached. "Mr. Ashcroft will do just fine."

His eyes flicker, just for a moment, and I tell myself that's a win.

"Take a seat." I gesture toward the back table, my hand steady even though my heart feels like it's trying to punch its way out of my chest. His lips twitch, just slightly, like he's amused.

Whatever game he's playing, I refuse to let him win. He gives a slight nod, his eyes never leaving mine. I turn on my heel before I do something really stupid—like react again.

"After you," he says, his voice soft but edged with something dangerous. I walk towards the table, every nerve on high alert, my breath coming in shallow bursts.

Come on, Lila. Up your game, bitch.

I square my shoulders, forcing my steps to stay steady, calm, in control. This is your cafe, your home turf. He's just a visitor—no matter how intimidating he looks in that perfectly tailored suit.

I settle into my chair, smoothing my blazer as I lift my chin and meet his gaze again. No blinking. No backing down.

"Shall we get started?" I say, my voice firm, even though my heart is still racing.

His lips curve ever so slightly. "By all means."

He leans back in his chair, watching me with an unsettling calm, his eyes flicking between my notes and my face like he's waiting to see which will crack first—my argument or my composure.

Not happening.

I let the silence sit, thick and heavy, letting it do half the work for me. Let him feel it. The weight of every set of eyes fixed on him. The weight of what he's here to destroy.

Ben Ashcroft expected a simple meeting. A polite discussion. Maybe a bit of push back.

He has no idea what he's walked into.

I square my shoulders, keeping my voice firm and clear. "Mr. Ashcroft, thank you for meeting with us today." I gesture around the table, making sure his attention follows mine. "We're here on behalf of The Silverbeck Business Alliance—a coalition of independent business owners, residents, and community leaders who will be directly impacted by your development project."

I push on. "We're here because we have serious concerns about your company's plans and before you say you understand, let me introduce you to the people whose livelihoods are at stake."

I turn to my right, nodding at Clara. "Clara is my co-lead

in this alliance. She owns The Willow Salon, a cornerstone of Silverbeck for over fifteen years."

Clara sits stiff-backed, arms folded over her chest, her expression polite but unwavering.

"Thomas Russell," I continue, motioning to the man beside her. "Runs Russell's Bakery, a family business that's been here for four generations."

Ben's gaze flickers briefly toward Thomas. The first crack in his polished detachment.

Thomas leans forward, folding his arms on the table. "I remember you, Ben," he says, his voice even but firm. "Knew your mother, too. She was a good woman. It's a damn shame to hear you've come back just to tear this place apart."

A few murmurs ripple around the table. I watch Ben closely, waiting for any sign of a reaction. A twitch of the jaw. A flicker of discomfort. Anything.

But he gives nothing away.

This is not the Ben I knew. Not even close and somehow, that's worse.

One by one, I introduce them—the butcher, the greengrocer, the art gallery owner. Fifteen business owners. A few community members. All here because they refuse to be erased.

Ben listens, impassive, hands folded neatly in front of him. Just calculation.

Finally, when I've named every single person in the room, I lean forward, resting my hands flat on the table.

"Now that you know who we are, Mr. Ashcroft," I say, my voice sharp but steady, "why don't you tell us exactly how you plan to justify ripping the heart out of this town?"

Silence.

For the first time since walking in, Ben exhales, slow and

measured. His eyes flick to mine, and for a second—just a second—I think I see something. A flicker of recognition. A sliver of hesitation.

Then it's gone.

The game begins.

I slide a neatly bound stack of reports across the table toward him. He doesn't even glance at it. His eyes stay locked on mine.

"Thank you, Ms Ng," he says, his lips curving into that faint, maddening smile again. "I'm always open to hearing community concerns."

Liar.

I suppress the urge to roll my eyes. We both know this meeting is more about appearances than solutions. He's here to pacify us, maybe throw out a few empty promises.

"We're not just here to express concerns. We want a solution that protects this community without sacrificing what makes it special."

Clara murmurs her agreement, and I hear Thomas mutter, "Exactly."

Ben leans back in his chair, tapping a finger thoughtfully on the table. "Collaboration is always… valuable," he says slowly. "But there are limits to what can be negotiated in business. Not everything can be preserved."

Translation: You can fight this all you want, but it won't change the outcome. The air crackles with unspoken tension. The quiet hum of the cafe feels deafening now, the espresso machine hissing softly in the background.

I refuse to blink. "We're asking for fairness. A development plan that considers the community you're affecting—not one that bulldozes over it without a second thought."

He tilts his head slightly, studying me like I'm a puzzle he's trying to solve. "Fairness is subjective. What one person sees as fairness, another sees as interference. Business decisions require pragmatism, not emotion."

My jaw tightens. The nerve of this man.

"We're not speaking emotionally," I counter. "We've backed everything with data—statistics on foot traffic, customer demographics, economic impact. All of which shows that small businesses like ours are crucial to the area's long-term stability."

I push the report toward him again. "It's all in there, if you'd like to verify."

He finally picks it up, flipping through the pages with maddening calmness. His lips twitch, but there's no humour in the expression—just calculation.

"Impressive work," he says, setting the report down with a soft thud. "But numbers don't always reflect reality. Sentiment can't be quantified, and nostalgia rarely pays the bills."

The words hit harder than they should, but I hold my ground.

"It's not nostalgia," I say evenly. "It's community. Something you seem to think is negotiable. It's not."

Clara leans in. "These businesses are our lives. Our homes."

Ben's gaze flicks to her, then back to me. For the briefest moment, something shifts in his expression—but just as quickly, his mask slides back into place.

"I understand that," he says, his voice as smooth as ever, but there's an unmistakable edge beneath it. "Which is why all businesses affected by the development will be financially compensated at a fair market price."

The words land like a calculated move—practiced, controlled. A statement meant to sound reasonable, even generous.

My chest tightens. He thinks money can fix this. Like a payout makes up for years of blood, sweat, and sacrifice. Like you can put a price tag on a legacy.

"Fair market price?" I repeat, forcing my voice to stay even. "Who decides what's fair? A corporate valuation team with no ties to this town? Numbers on a spreadsheet that don't account for history, for loyalty, for the community that depends on these businesses?"

A muscle ticks in his jaw, but he doesn't take the bait. "Compensation ensures that no one walks away with nothing."

Clara scoffs. "We don't want to walk away at all."

Ben exhales slowly, like he's explaining something obvious to a stubborn child. "I respect what you've built here, but progress requires movement. No one is being forced out without options."

This isn't about options. It's about erasure.

Thomas exhales sharply, shaking his head. "You think throwing money at us makes it better? You really have been gone too long, Ben."

"I don't expect everyone to be happy with change. But this project isn't about pushing people out—it's about growth. The town benefits in the long run."

I let out a quiet laugh, shaking my head. "Growth for who? Certainly not the businesses you're displacing. Not the families who rely on them." I lean forward, my hands pressing against the cool surface of the table. "Tell me, Mr. Ashcroft—why Silverbeck? There are plenty of other areas nearby that are better suited for large-scale developments. So why here?"

He remains perfectly neutral. "Because Silverbeck presents the best opportunity."

"For your investors," I correct. "Not for the people who live here."

His jaw tightens slightly, a flicker of something behind his eyes—annoyance? Amusement?

"There are factors at play that go beyond sentiment," he replies smoothly. "Infrastructure, accessibility, projected returns—this location made the most sense."

I tilt my head, studying him. "You expect us to just... accept that? To sit back while you wipe out the businesses that make this town what it is?"

He exhales, slow and measured. "I expect you to understand that change is inevitable and that no one here is being left without options."

"Options?" Paul, the hardware store owner, scoffs. "Being bought out isn't an option. It's a last resort."

Clara folds her arms. "A fair market price doesn't replace thirty years of building relationships, of customers who trust us, of livelihoods passed down through generations."

Ben doesn't flinch. "It ensures stability. A fresh start. An opportunity to reinvest elsewhere."

A fresh start. Like the one he gave himself when he left this town behind.

I inhale sharply, forcing my voice to stay steady. "What about the people who can't just pick up and start over? The ones who have nowhere else to go? Who built their entire lives here, only to have it taken from them in the name of 'growth'?"

His gaze darkens, the faintest flicker of something beneath the surface—hesitation? Regret? But then it's gone, smoothed over with that infuriating corporate calm.

The cafe falls silent again, the weight of my words hanging between us.

His gaze sharpens, a flicker of something darker flashing in his eyes. He opens his mouth to respond, but Thomas cuts in.

"You've got all the power here," Thomas says, his tone gruff but steady. "We get that. But power doesn't mean you can't do the right thing."

Ben pauses, his eyes narrowing ever so slightly, before leaning back in his chair once more. Ben's fingers drum once against the table, his expression unreadable. The weight of the room presses in, thick with tension. He exhales, slow and deliberate, then reaches down beside him.

A sleek black briefcase clicks open.

I watch as he methodically pulls out a neat stack of envelopes—each one thick, heavy, the kind of thing that carries finality inside.

My stomach tightens. What now?

"I understand emotions are running high," Ben says smoothly, completely composed once again. "But I'm not here to debate sentiment."

He places a stack of envelopes onto the table.

"These contain further details on the development," Ben continues. "Along with individual offers for each business owner affected. You'll find that they are..." He pauses, just long enough for it to feel intentional. "...generous. More than fair market value."

A hush settles over the room. The rustling of envelopes being picked up, the hesitant glances exchanged.

I don't look away from him. I won't.

"This isn't a negotiation," I say flatly.

He tilts his head, as if considering. "It's a choice."

I scoff. Bullshit.

Ben rises from his chair, buttoning his suit jacket with a practiced, effortless motion. He's already decided he's done here.

"I won't pressure anyone," he says, his voice smooth, measured. "You have time to consider your options."

Options. As if there really are any.

He adjusts his cufflinks, casting a brief, sweeping glance across the room. No urgency. No concern. Just cool, calculated detachment.

I grip the edges of the envelope in front of me, but I don't open it.

"What's the deadline?" Paul asks, his voice rough.

Ben turns slightly, his gaze flicking to him. "Ten days."

A murmur ripples through the group. Ten days? That's nothing.

Thomas exhales sharply, shaking his head. "You really are your father's son."

A sharp silence follows.

Something flashes in Ben's eyes. Something dangerous.

For a second, just a second, his mask nearly slips. But then, he exhales through his nose, tightens his jaw, and chooses not to react.

"I'll take everything under advisement," he says finally, his tone measured but distant. "I trust you'll make the right decision." His eyes lingering on me a fraction too long. "Until next time, Ms Ng."

He turns, not waiting for an answer. Not lingering. Just walking away.

The door swings shut behind him.

The silence he leaves behind is almost suffocating.

He's gone. But the damage isn't.

---

The business owners linger for a while, murmuring amongst

themselves, the weight of Ben's bombshell still pressing down on the room. No one opens their envelopes. Not yet. Not here.

Thomas grumbles under his breath, arms crossed tightly over his chest. "Damn shame," he mutters. "He was always a sweet kid."

A few people nod in agreement, but no one knows what else to say. Eventually, one by one, they start to leave, clutching their envelopes like they weigh a ton. I don't breathe properly until the door clicks shut behind the last one.

Finally, it's just me and my friends.

I grip the edge of the table, trying to steady my breathing, my heart still racing.

Olivia's voice cuts through the quiet.

"What. The. Hell. Was that?"

"Yeah," Sophie adds, eyes wide. "Do you know him?"

I hesitate, my pulse kicking up again. Do I tell them the truth?

I glance at the door, half expecting him to walk back in. No. Not yet.

I force a laugh, shaking my head. "No. Of course not. He's just... intense."

Sophie narrows her eyes.

"It's nothing," I say quickly, grabbing the stack of papers and pretending to organize them. "It's just business."

I grab the stack of papers, straightening them with trembling hands. *Keep moving. Keep it together.*

My vision blurs. My pulse pounds. I need out—now.

"Excuse me," I force a small smile and gesture toward the back. "I just need a minute."

I barely wait for their response before heading toward the bathroom, my steps brisk and my heart hammering against my ribs.

The second the door clicks shut behind me, I grip the edge of the sink, my breath coming in ragged gasps. The floodgates open.

He's really here.

My mind spirals, my worst fears unravelling in front of me. He hates me and now he's come back to destroy what's left of my life—my mum's business, the cafe, everything we've worked so hard to build. I grip the sink, blinking fast. Not now. Not here. But the hurt crashes in anyway. Get it together, Lila. You can fall apart later—when you're home, alone, and safe from questions you can't answer.

I take a deep breath and splash cold water on my face, the chill jolting me back to reality. I glance in the mirror, brushing away the stray tears that cling stubbornly to my lashes. My eyes are red-rimmed, my cheeks flushed, but I'm calmer now. Composed.

Almost.

I fix my ponytail, straighten my blazer, and take one last breath before stepping back into the cafe. Everything's fine. No one needs to know.

But the second I walk out, Willow and Sophie are waiting for me, their eyes filled with concern.

"You okay?" Willow asks softly, her gaze scanning my face.

"Yeah," I say too quickly, forcing a smile that feels more like a grimace. "I'm fine. It's just... stress. You know how it is."

"Lila," Sophie says, stepping closer and placing a hand on my arm. "You don't have to pretend with us. Whatever is going on, we're here."

For a moment, I consider telling them everything—the truth about Ben—but the words stick in my throat. Not now. Not yet.

Instead, I nod and take a breath. "Thanks. I just needed a

minute to regroup."

Sophie smiles gently. "Take all the time you need. We've got your back."

Olivia nods. "Always."

Their support should make me feel lighter, but the knot in my chest only tightens. Because I know this isn't over. Not even close.

#  5

## Ben

I step out of the cafe; the door swinging shut behind me with a soft click, but the tension follows me out like a shadow. The scent of coffee and roses lingers in the air, clinging to my skin, as if I haven't truly left.

Lila.

I've sat through hundreds of business meetings—some tense, some brutal, some downright hostile. But none of them felt like this.

None of them left me so off-balance.

I hadn't planned to play it that cold. I told myself on the way up here that I'd acknowledge her, keep it polite, light—acknowledge our past without getting lost in it. Maybe even throw in a wry comment, something that said I remembered everything but wasn't holding onto it.

But then I walked in, saw her standing there, a goddess—composed, fierce, her eyes already locked on me—and I choked.

My instincts kicked in—cold, controlled, professional. It's what I do best.

Now it just feels like shit.

## BEN

I saw it. The flicker of recognition in her eyes, the way her lips parted like she was about to say something.

Then it was gone.

The light dimmed, her guard snapping back into place so fast it was almost a physical thing. Her shoulders tightened, her eyes hardened, and she smiled that perfectly polite, distant smile—the same one I'd given her.

It hit harder than it should have.

I rake a hand through my hair, exhaling sharply. **Fifteen years, and this place still gets under my skin.**

I used to stand at Thomas' counter after school, eating sticky buns while he and my mum talked. Back then, he smiled at me— warm, familiar. Today, he barely looked at me. His words echo in my head—*You really are your father's son.* My jaw tightens. It took everything in me not to reach across the table and shut him up right then and there.

Something tightens in my chest. **Guilt.** I shove it aside, but it lingers.

But one thing gnawed at me throughout the entire meeting: Lila.

*Lila Ng.*

I glanced at her left hand more times than I want to admit, my brain circling back like a dog chasing its tail.

No ring. No tan line. Nothing.

But that doesn't mean anything. Not everyone wears a ring. Maybe she takes it off when she works. Maybe her husband doesn't care if she wears one. Maybe he's the kind of man who lets his wife fight his battles while he sits on the sidelines.

That thought pisses me off more than it should.

If she's married, where the hell was he? A real man would've been here, standing beside her. Protecting what's his.

I would've been.

The idea of meeting him—of sizing up the man who married her, who gets to wake up beside her, touch her, know her in ways I never did—sent something dark and ugly twisting in my gut.

I have no right to care.

But I do.

I've been with more women than I care to admit—beautiful, intelligent, completely unattached. Women who knew the rules, who never asked for more than I could give. It was easy. Simple.

Lila is neither of those things.

No one else has ever made my chest tighten with just a glance. No one else has ever made my pulse spike with a single word.

No one else was *her*.

I wasn't supposed to come back after today. One meeting. Hear them out. Nod politely. Move on. That was the plan—clean, simple, no mess.

Then she looked at me.

Sharp. Unshakable and yet, something simmered beneath that perfectly controlled exterior.

I've told myself for years that leaving was the only way. That it was for the best. That she was better off without me. I want to know if she's happy. If she hates me as much as I hate myself for what I did. If someone else stepped in and gave her the life she deserved.

I *need* to know.

Where was he? Her husband. A woman like her doesn't stay single, but I never go after married women. Never.

But I can't leave without looking him in the eye. Without knowing he treats her right. That he's *worthy* of her.

By the time I reach my car, the decision is already made.

I'll see her again.

Not for the project. Not for business.

For her.

I fish my phone out of my pocket and scroll to Claire's number.

She answers on the second ring. Efficient as always. "Mr Ashcroft?"

"Claire, book me the penthouse at the best hotel near the site."

Keys clack on her keyboard. "Kingsley Hotel."

"Send me the confirmation."

"Anything else?"

"No," I say, already picturing the suite's floor-to-ceiling windows and the peace of being alone while I plan my next move.

"Enjoy your stay," Claire says before the line clicks off.

I stare at my phone for a second longer, then slip it back into my pocket and climb into the car.

I shake my head, smirking despite myself. You're playing with fire.

Worst of all?

You've already decided you like the burn.

# 6

## Lila

The offer was insulting—below market value, like we'd be too stupid or desperate to notice. A slap in the face after everything we've built and of course, he delivered it with that infuriating calm—like he was doing us a favour. What's really driving me mad is how much space he's taking up in my head. The way he looked at me like a stranger. It's ridiculous. I should be focused on the fight ahead, not getting thrown off balance by a man I haven't seen in fifteen years.

Not letting old feelings tangle up with new fury.

Damn it, Lila. Get a grip.

The bell above the door chimes, and every muscle in my body locks up.

No. No fucking way.

But there he is. Ben Ashcroft, standing in the doorway like he owns the place. His eyes scan the room until they land on me. He's not in a suit today, but somehow, that's worse. Fitted navy shirt rolled to the elbows, tailored trousers, an expensive watch glinting from his wrist. He looks ridiculously put together for someone who should have no business showing up here again.

*What the hell is he doing here?*

I fight the instinct to bolt and keep my expression neutral as he strides toward the counter. My pulse kicks up anyway.

"Good morning," he says, his voice just as smooth, just as irritatingly confident as it was yesterday. "Thought I'd stop in for coffee."

I fold my arms, narrowing my eyes. "Doing some early reconnaissance before you knock the place down?"

Ben chuckles softly, like he's actually amused. "If I wanted to knock it down, I wouldn't need coffee first."

"Right." I tilt my head, giving him a tight smile. "Coffee. Because there's absolutely nowhere else in the city to get one, is there?"

His eyes glint, and he leans just a little closer over the counter. Too close.

"I wanted to apologize," he says, his voice soft but deliberate.

"Oh, so you've decided to cancel the plans after all?"

He blinks, caught off guard for a split second, before his lips curl into a faint smile. "No."

"Shame," I say, folding my arms. "That might've made this conversation more interesting."

Ben chuckles softly, recovering far too quickly. "I was... surprised to see you," he continues, his eyes never leaving mine. "Didn't handle it the way I should've. It's been a long time, and I'd like to—" He pauses, a faint smile curving his lips—too polished to be innocent.

"Start again."

The words hit harder than they should, echoing in my head, swirling around like smoke I can't quite clear.

*Start again.*

Does he mean *now*? Or fifteen years ago, when he walked

away without so much as a goodbye? Mt stomach tightens. It's too much, all at once, and for a split second, I can't speak.

But then I remember who he is now. Ben Ashcroft, the man trying to take away everything I've built.

He rests his hand on the counter, the tendons flexing beneath his tanned skin, forearm corded with muscle. He leans in slightly, close enough that I catch the faint scent of his cologne—dark, expensive, with just a hint of something warm and masculine.

The air feels heavier, warmer. His fitted shirt stretches across broad shoulders, emphasizing just how much he's changed since the scrappy, reckless boy I once knew.

"It's good to see you again, Lila," he says—his voice soft, low, and deliberate, sending a ripple of something unsettling down my spine. My breath stutters, heat coiling low in my stomach. No. Not this time.

"Oh, so you do remember me. How unexpected."

"Some things are hard to forget."

"Funny," I say, my voice sharp, "you didn't seem to remember me at all before." I fold my arms, tilting my head.

The smirk fades from his face, replaced by something quieter, almost hesitant. His eyes soften, that familiar confidence dimming just a little. "I deserved that," he admits, his voice lower, almost regretful.

His gaze lingers on me for a beat too long, his brow furrowing slightly. "It was the name that threw me. Ng, not Lau." He tilts his head.

My breath catches.

"I got married," I say, the words slipping out before I can stop them.

What the actual fuck, Lila?!

Ben's body tenses, his jaw tightening so fast it looks painful. His eyes flick to my left hand—bare, glaringly bare—then back to my face. The softness is gone, replaced by something darker.

His nostrils flare, his jaw clenching. "I figured." His voice is dangerously low, his smile gone.

Shit. I should backtrack, but it's too late now and my pride kicks in full force. "Happily married," I say, too bright, too steady. His lips press into a thin line, his eyes glinting with something sharp, something raw. His knuckles whiten as his hand curls into a fist on the counter. He forces a slow, deliberate breath through his nose, but it doesn't quite mask the storm in his eyes.

"He's a very lucky man," Ben says, his voice low and clipped. Controlled. But I don't miss the edge beneath it—the bite hiding behind the words.

I cross my arms, willing my heart to slow down. "Yep," I say again, popping the 'p' like I've got everything under control.

His eyes drop to my left hand—lingering. "Where's your ring?"

The question slices through the air. Casual tone, but his eyes are sharp. Waiting.

My brain scrambles. "I... I don't wear it when I'm working," I blurt. "It's impractical."

Ben lets out a soft chuckle, but there's nothing warm about it. "Right. Wouldn't want to risk damaging something so... precious."

The silence between us crackles like static. His eyes don't move from mine. I grip the counter tighter, trying to ignore the flush creeping up my neck.

Keep it together, Lila. Don't crack now.

"Well," I say, straightening, trying for nonchalance. "Can I take your order?"

My voice is steady, but inside I'm scrambling, desperate to push this conversation back to safe territory.

He pauses, his eyes searching mine for a beat longer than I'm comfortable with. Then, he nods, slipping back into that calm, composed shell. "Black coffee. No milk. No sugar."

Of course.

I nod, grabbing a cup and turning to the coffee machine. "Black coffee. Got it."

I pour the coffee into the cup, the rich, dark liquid swirling as I set it down in front of him. "One black coffee. No milk, no sugar."

He picks it up, smiling slightly. "Simple."

"Convenient," I say flatly. "Well—enjoy."

I'm already halfway turned toward the register, hoping he'll take the hint, but his voice stops me cold. "Actually," he says casually, "I'll have something sweet too. Cake, maybe."

I glance back over my shoulder. "Seriously?"

His smile widens. "Your recommendation."

Of course he wants to drag this out.

I sigh, turning toward the display case. "Matcha chiffon. It's light, fluffy, a little bitter. Not for everyone."

His gaze flicks to the cake, then to me. "Good thing I've never been afraid of a challenge."

Cocky bastard.

I grab a plate and cut a slice, setting it down on the counter with more force than necessary. "Enjoy it—or don't. Makes no difference to me."

He takes the plate, but lingers—eyes on me, not the cake. Watching. Waiting. I hate that a stupid slice of cake feels like a power move.

"Thanks," he says, his lips curving into that maddening smirk.

I cross my arms, refusing to give him more than a bored expression. "That'll be £9.20."

He slides a twenty-pound note across the counter, his eyes never leaving mine. "Keep the change."

"Generous," I mutter, putting the change in the Guide dogs for the blind collection pot next to the till.

"Always," he replies smoothly, taking a sip of his coffee.

For a second, the air between us thickens, heavy with unspoken tension. But I don't crack. I keep my face calm, unreadable.

"Anything else?" I ask flatly.

His gaze lingers. "Not today."

He turns toward the door, but just before he steps outside, he glances back over his shoulder.

"I meant it, you know," he says softly, his voice low and deliberate. "It really is good to see you again."

Then he's gone, the bell above the door chiming softly as it swings shut.

The cafe falls quiet, his presence lingering like the scent of dark roast and his cologne—deep, warm, and annoyingly hard to ignore.

I grip the counter, my heart pounding harder than it should. What the hell is his game?

Fortunately, the day doesn't give me much time to dwell on it. The door swings open again, and a flood of customers pours in—a mix of regulars and students with laptops, already eyeing the best seats.

I inhale deeply, forcing a smile as I serve one cappuccino after another, grateful for the constant hum of activity. The orders come in fast—americano, latte, oat milk flat white.

It's easier this way. Busier is better. Busier means less time to think about him, about the strange tension lingering between us, or the way his voice sounded just a little too sincere when he said it was good to see me.

I clear a table, tossing crumpled napkins into the bin with more force than necessary. Focus, Lila. Focus on what matters—Bloom and Brew, keeping everything afloat.

5 o'clock.

I yank open the supply cupboard, needing something—anything—to distract me. Flour. Sugar. Rice flour. Perfect. I'll bake something for tomorrow. Keep my hands busy so my brain doesn't have time to spiral.

I grab my mum's old recipe for *nian gao*, her favourite sticky rice cake. Mum always makes *nian gao* during Spring Festival. It's supposed to bring good luck, right now we need all the luck we can get. I start mixing the ingredients. The motions are soothing, familiar, grounding me in a way that nothing else has since the moment Ben walked through that door. It's ancient history. So what if he's back? You're a grown woman, not some heartbroken teenager.

As I stir the batter, the sweet scent of the nian gao fills the air, tugging me back to that spring afternoon.

*We're at school, sitting on a sun-warmed bench. Ben's shoulders slump, his usual confidence replaced by a shy, almost embarrassed look.*

*"I forgot my lunch," he mutters, kicking at the gravel beneath his feet.*

*I dig into my bag and pull out a small container. My mum's nian gao, still warm.*

*"Here," I offer, holding it out to him.*

*He looks at it, then at me, brow furrowed. "What's that?"*

*"Nian gao. It's sticky rice cake. My mum made it this morning."*

*He hesitates for a second, then takes it, breaking off a piece and popping it into his mouth. His eyes light up.*

*"Damn, that's good," he says around a mouthful.*

*I laugh, relief flooding through me—until I hear the snickers from behind us.*

*"Gross," someone mutters. "Weird Asian food."*

*My stomach twists, heat rising in my cheeks, but before I can say anything, Ben turns to them, his jaw set.*

*"Shut the hell up," he says, his voice sharp and confident again. "It's better than whatever crap you're eating."*

*They go quiet, walking away with annoyed glances, and I suddenly like him even more than I already did.*

*That was the beginning.*

Now, it's the end.

I snap back to the present, blinking at the bowl of batter in front of me. My chest tightens, the weight of everything pressing down on me. I pour the batter into a pan and slide it into the oven, taking a deep breath to steady myself.

Footsteps shuffle behind me.

"Mum," I say, glancing over my shoulder. "You should finish early. I'll close up."

She frowns. "Are you sure, love? I don't mind staying."

"I'm sure," I say, giving her a small smile. "You've been on your feet all day. Go home, get some rest."

She hesitates, then nods. "Okay. But don't stay too late."

"I won't."

She grabs her coat and leaves, the door closing softly behind her.

I glance toward the ceiling. The flat above the cafe is everything to us—affordable, convenient, and close enough that my mum doesn't have to travel far. We can't lose this place. We wouldn't find anything else like it in this area, not with our budget and Ben wants to take it away.

I feel sick just thinking about it. I grab a cloth and start wiping down the counter, scrubbing harder than necessary, hoping to burn off the frustration bubbling inside me.

The bell above the door chimes.

"We're closed," I call out without looking up.

"I'm not here for coffee."

The air shifts—charged, heavy—I don't need to turn around to know it's him.

Still, I turn slowly, already bracing myself.

Ben stands just inside the door, his tall frame soaking up space like he owns it, hands shoved casually into his pockets.

"I smelled something... familiar," he says, his gaze flicking to the tray of *nian gao* cooling on the counter. "Thought I'd drop in." He says it like it's nothing, but I catch the flicker in his eyes. I shove it down before it can soften me.

I raise an eyebrow. "As I said, we're closed and these aren't for sale."

Ben pulls out his wallet, casually sliding a £10 note onto the counter. "One slice."

"No."

He takes a step closer. "Come on, Lila. Just one slice."

He adds another £10 note on top of the first. His voice is calm, deliberate.

I cross my arms, narrowing my eyes at him. "You think throwing money around is going to change my mind?"

"£50," he counters smoothly, placing the note like a chess move. "You're running a business. Seems like a smart deal."

"It's not about the money," I say, my jaw tightening.

His lips twitch into a smirk. "It always is."

"Not to me," I snap.

"£100," he says, his voice dropping dangerously low. He leans on the counter, closing the space between us. "For one slice."

My heart races at his proximity, but I stand my ground, refusing to let him see how much he's affecting me.

"Offer me a thousand—I'd still say no." I say, stepping back. His eyes darken with something that looks suspiciously like respect—or maybe it's something else entirely.

"Money can't buy everything, Ben."

A beat of silence stretches between us, thick with tension. He tucks the money back into his wallet, that smirk softening into something more thoughtful. "You've always been stubborn."

"I prefer determined," I say, my voice steady.

He chuckles softly, backing toward the door. "I'll be back," he says, his voice a low promise. "You've got something I want."

"The buyout is a joke so you can save your breath. The answer's still no."

He stops at the door, his fingers resting lightly on the frame, a wicked glint sparking in his gaze. "I'm not talking about the buyout."

My breath catches, heat spreading through my chest, my pulse thrumming in my ears. I'm caught in the weight of his stare, my mind spinning in directions it shouldn't.

What the hell is he talking about?

I blink, snapping myself out of it, my voice sharper than I intend. "Whatever it is, you're not getting that either."

His lips curve into a slow, knowing smile. "We'll see."

Just like that, he's gone—the door swinging shut behind him, leaving me slightly breathless.

The cafe feels too warm, my skin still buzzing. His aftershave—dark, warm, mixed with coffee—lingers like a goddamn invitation. It shouldn't affect me. But it does. *What the hell was that?*

He's trying to charm me. The fucker is trying to woo me into changing my mind. Dirty tactics, pure and simple.

I clench my jaw, my pulse spiking again, but this time from anger. If he thinks I'm that easy to manipulate, he's in for a rude awakening.

I hate him. I really do.

But my body?

It hasn't gotten the memo.

Business, my ass.

# 7

## Ben

Lila—challenging me with every sarcastic smile, every sharp remark. Grounded. Stubborn. Impossible to ignore.

"Happily married."

The words keep echoing in my head, sharp and jarring, like a punch to the gut I didn't see coming.

My hand grips the steering wheel tighter as I drive back to the hotel. She said it so easily, too easily, like she's been waiting for this moment to throw it in my face. I pride myself on keeping calm under pressure, but hearing her say those two words made my chest feel like it was caving in.

Why does it bother me so much? It's been fifteen years.

I step into the penthouse suite at the Kingsley Hotel, tossing my jacket onto the chair by the window. The skyline stretches out before me, glittering and cold.

Nottingham isn't my city anymore. It's a relic of a past I left behind, a place filled with memories I've spent years burying. London is my empire now—bigger, faster, richer. Everything I've built is there, every move carefully calculated, every piece of my life exactly where it belongs.

Lila would never fit into that world. She's too rooted, preferring flour-dusted counters and well-worn books over sleek offices and rooftop bars. What the hell am I doing picturing that? She's married—for God's sake.

I head straight to the drinks cabinet, grabbing the bottle of whisky without thinking. The familiar clink of glass against glass follows as I pour a double—just enough to take the edge off. I knock it back in one go. It burns all the way down, but not enough. Not nearly enough. My fingers curl around the empty glass, jaw tightening at the thought of some faceless man waiting for her at home, living the life I walked away from. A life that should've been mine.

I shouldn't care. It shouldn't matter.

I glance around the penthouse, trying to ground myself in anything but the spiral in my head. It's a stunning space—sleek lines, polished surfaces, the kind of luxury most people spend their lives chasing. Every inch screams wealth and taste.

Well... almost every inch.

My eyes catch on a peculiar object perched on a side console near the fireplace—a ceramic duck. Hand-painted, antique, and completely out of place amid all the modern opulence. I frown, stepping closer. It's got this oddly judgmental look on its face, like it's silently appraising me. Or mocking me.

Weird choice. Hotel designer's idea of eclectic charm? Or maybe the owner's got a strange sense of humour.

I snort under my breath.

"Ey up, me duck." Fitting, I suppose—welcome back to Nottingham.

But even that ridiculous bird can't distract me for long. The thought still gnaws at me, sharp and relentless.

I pace toward the window, my pulse thrumming in my

ears. Lila. She was mine once. Every laugh, every late-night conversation, every quiet moment under the stars. Mine.

I was her first.

Her first kiss. Her first everything. I was the one who made her blush, who held her when she was scared, who kissed her until she forgot how to breathe.

Now she's his.

The thought of him—whoever the hell he is—having any part of her makes my stomach twist. Did he whisper promises to her the way I did? Did she believe him like she believed me?

Some spineless bastard who lets her family run a cafe and florist alone while he coasts through life? She's breaking her back, and he just stands by?

My jaw tightens, rage simmering. He should be supporting her, not watching her struggle.

Does he even see her? The way she straightens when she's tired, still smiling through it all because she's too proud to ask for help?

If it were me, she wouldn't lift a finger unless she wanted to. No rent, no stress—I'd give her everything.

Everything.

My fists clench, nails biting into my palms. Fuck that.

I pull out my phone and scroll to Shaw's number—best private investigator money can buy. I haven't needed him in a while, but tonight, I want answers.

He picks up on the second ring. "Ashcroft."

"I need a job done," I say, my voice flat. "I want everything you can find on Lila Ng's husband."

There's a pause. "Her husband?"

"Yes. Name, occupation, income, criminal record—if he's

ever gotten a parking ticket, I want to know. Every last detail and I want it fast."

"I'll get started right away."

"You've got twenty-four hours. Sooner, if you're smart."

"I understand."

I hang up without another word and toss the phone on the table. This isn't curiosity anymore—it's strategy and if her husband's even half the man he should be...

I'll find out soon enough.

I shouldn't be this worked up. This was supposed to be simple. Hear them out. Offer money. Close the deal.

Not... this.

The tension coils tighter in my chest, sharp and unrelenting. I scrub a hand over my face and head toward the bathroom, stripping off my shirt on the way. Maybe a cold shower will cut through this knot in my gut, shake off the heat crawling beneath my skin.

The water hits like ice—bracing, punishing—but it still doesn't chase her from my mind.

I brace a hand against the tiled wall, exhaling hard. It's been a while since I've been with anyone. Maybe that's all this is— too long without a distraction, without someone in my bed. Maybe that's why the sight of her—those eyes, that mouth, that voice—hit like a wrecking ball.

Still, it doesn't explain the way her voice loops in my head. Or the way her fake smile cut sharper than anything else today.

I stay under the water longer than I should, hoping to feel clean, clear, composed.

But when I step out and dry off, the knot's still there. Tight. Twisting.

The email from Shaw comes in just as I'm pouring another

drink. My laptop pings, and I cross the room, ice clinking in the glass as I lean over to read it.

The subject line: Lila Ng.

My pulse kicks up as I open it.

The cafe, the florist, the flat above it. Tight margins. Her mum's health—hospital visits, prescriptions. But one line stands out like a beacon—no marriage certificate. No divorce records.

She lied.

I reread it. Twice.

Relief hits first. Then something darker. Why lie? To push me away? Test me? Or just to see how I'd react?

My fingers tighten around the glass, the sharp scent of whiskey cutting through the air as my chest loosens. I pace back toward the window, the city lights below glinting like broken glass. Lila was always good at keeping me on my toes.

But this? This was a calculated move.

If she wants to play games, I'll play along.

I down the rest of my drink, my thoughts swirling, half-formed plans already taking shape in my mind.

I grab my phone and dial Claire. She answers on the first ring.

"Mr Ashcroft?"

"I need a delivery sent to Lila Ng at the cafe," I say, my voice calm, deliberate. "A gift set. Two coffee mugs—Mr and Mrs"

Claire pauses. "Would you like a note attached?"

A slow smile spreads across my face. Perfect.

"'For you and ...him. I hope he likes matcha.'"

"Understood. I'll arrange it for tomorrow."

"Good, Claire?" I pause, my grip tightening on the phone. "Increase the offer by 10%. I want it on her desk by noon."

"Yes, sir."

I hang up, slipping the phone back into my pocket as a slow smile spreads across my face.

She thinks she's in control. But I always win.

Still... a flicker of doubt creeps in, sharp and unwelcome.

What if she doesn't bite?

What if she sees right through it—and walks away for good?

I shove the thought aside. No. She won't. She's too proud, too stubborn, too curious not to react and maybe that's the point.

Maybe I want her to react.

I glance at the window again, watching the city lights blur into amber smears against the glass. Whatever this is between us—it's not over. Not even close.

Tomorrow, the game changes.

\*\*\*\*

I go back to the cafe again.

Twice in one day. Pathetic, really.

But it's not about the cafe anymore. It's about her. The scent hit me the second I walked through the door—sweet, warm, familiar. Sticky rice, caramelised sugar. For a split second, I'm sixteen again, sitting on that sun-warmed bench while she shares her lunch with me.

Warm nian gao, nervous eyes, soft smiles.

She made me feel seen—like I wasn't just some invisible kid from the wrong side of town. The cake was good. But she was better.

That's what the nian gao is—a piece of her. A piece of us. A life I haven't let myself think about in years and now I'm standing here, watching her across the counter, trying to buy it off her like some rich prick.

£50 then £100, £200.

Everyone in my world has a price. Everyone. Deals, negotiations, contracts—it's just a matter of numbers. But her?

She didn't budge.

Maybe a part of me wanted her to. Wanted her to be like everyone else, just so I could stop feeling like she's the only person I can't get under control.

But she's not like them.

That's what makes me want her more than anything.

# 8

# Lila

The cafe hums with life, the scent of fresh roses, eucalyptus, and lilies mingling with coffee and the faint aroma of cinnamon. Vases clutter the worktables, half-finished bouquets in various stages of completion for Sophie and Marcus's charity gala.

Maeve perches on a stool, her tiny tongue sticking out in concentration as she draws tulips on small cards. Her red and yellow flowers dance across the paper with surprising precision for a four-year-old.

"They're tulips," Maeve announces proudly, holding one up. "Mummy says they're special for people with Parkinson's."

"They are," I say, crouching next to her. "You're doing an amazing job."

Olivia leans down to kiss her daughter's head. "She's been obsessed with tulips and their meanings lately."

"Because tulips are magic," Maeve says seriously, like she's revealing the secret to the universe.

The bell on the cafe door jingles, and my mum bustles in from the back, balancing a tray of freshly steamed baos and a pot of tea. "Lila, have you even offered your friends anything?

Honestly, what kind of hostess are you?"

I sigh, but before I can reply, Sophie perks up. "Auntie Mei, you always know exactly what we need." I don't miss the warmth that blooms in my chest at the way they call her that—like she's theirs too. Like family. It's been years since I had a support system outside Mum. My old friends moved on—different cities, different lives—and for a long time, I thought that part of my world was done.

When I first joined Books That Bang, it was just meant to be a fun escape. A place to meet people who actually liked reading spicy books like me, nothing more. I never imagined I'd find such a great bunch of women—funny, fierce, loyal—who somehow feel like home. Like I belong again.

Mum beams, setting the tray down in the centre of the table. "Of course, you girls work too hard. You need to eat!" She starts pouring tea with practiced precision, already fussing over Maeve, who's kneeling on a chair, doodling intensely on a stack of cards.

"Are those tulips, sweetheart?" Mum asks, brushing Maeve's curls out of her face.

Maeve nods, her little hands gripping a crayon. "Tulips mean hope," she says matter-of-factly. Sophie reaches over, giving Maeve's tiny hand a gentle squeeze. "That's right, sweetheart. My dad is going to love them."

Olivia presses a kiss to the top of Maeve's head. "When she heard about the tulip's symbol, she wanted to make these for the event."

I glance at the stack of handmade cards spread across the table—each one decorated with Maeve's careful crayon work, bright tulips in shades of red, yellow, and pink. "They're beautiful," I say honestly. "We'll make sure they go on every table."

Maeve grins, clearly pleased with herself, then turns her attention back to her masterpiece. Mum starts refilling cups like she's hosting a formal tea ceremony. "You all work so hard for this event—you need your strength." Then, her eyes narrow slightly as she turns to me. "Lila, don't think I haven't noticed you barely eating today."

"Mum—"

She clucks her tongue, placing a bao directly on my plate. "Eat."

Willow smothers a laugh behind her cup. Olivia shoots me a teasing look. "I think that was a direct order."

I sigh, tearing off a piece of the bao. "You all enjoy this way too much."

"Obviously," Sophie quips, popping a dumpling into her mouth. The conversation drifts as we sort through the floral arrangements for the charity event. Mum fusses over the details, making sure the bouquets are just right, while Maeve turns her attention to the bouquets. "Maeve, sweetheart," Olivia says, gently prying a clump of baby's breath from her tiny hands. "We're trying to make it pretty, not... abstract."

Maeve pouts. "But the flowers are fighting. They want to be together!"

Sophie laughs from the counter. "Future floral artist in the making. Watch out, Lila."

I force a smile, but tension lingers beneath it. I've been on edge all day, ever since it arrived—the envelope with Ashcroft Holdings stamped across the front. It sits on the counter, taunting me, waiting to be opened.

Not yet.

"Lila," Olivia calls out, pulling me from my thoughts. "We

need more greenery for the centrepieces. Where's that eucalyptus?"

I nod, grabbing a bundle from the worktable and handing it to her. "Here. You've got this, bossy."

She grins. "Someone has to keep this operation running smoothly."

Willow, ever the voice of calm reason, quietly finishes tying bows around the vases. "The gala is going to look beautiful. Sophie, your dad's going to be so proud."

Sophie's smile softens. "I hope so. He's had a rough year. This fundraiser means a lot to him."

A pang of emotion hits me, and I'm grateful for the distraction of the flowers. I know how much this event means to Sophie, how much her dad's battle with Parkinson's has shaped her life. This isn't just about raising money—it's about hope.

"I'm glad we could help," I say, my voice steady even though my chest tightens. "Your dad deserves a night like this."

Sophie squeezes my hand briefly before turning back to her task.

Olivia, on the other hand, has already eyed the envelope on the counter like it's about to explode. "Are you really going to ignore that all night?"

I glance at the envelope, my stomach twisting. "I'm thinking about it."

"Don't." Olivia walks over and hands me the envelope. "Open it. Let's see what the devil himself is up to now."

I hesitate, fingers brushing over the paper.

"Lila?" Her voice is soft, laced with concern. "What's going on?"

I clench my jaw. "It's another offer."

Mum walks over, wiping her hands on her apron. "Let me

see."

I hesitate. "Mum—"

But she's already plucking the envelope from my grip, her brows knitting together as she pulls out the letter. Silence stretches as she reads, her expression shifting from confusion to shock. Her lips part slightly. "This... is more than last time."

"How much more?" I ask, my throat suddenly dry.

Mum's eyes flick back to the paper, scanning the numbers again like they might change. "Ten per cent more," she says, barely above a whisper.

You've got to be kidding me.

The air in the cafe stills.

Willow lets out a low whistle. "Wow. That's..." she struggles for the word, before settling on, "disappointing."

My jaw clenches, heat rising up my spine. Of course, he'd do this. Ben actually thinks we're desperate enough to take this? I should have seen it coming.

"It's an insult," Olivia mutters, shaking her head. "Like throwing pocket change at a problem and expecting it to go away."

I can feel my mum's gaze on me before she even speaks.

"It's not... a terrible amount," she says gently, her voice careful, her fingers smoothing over the edge of the letter. "It's more than we've ever had in savings."

A heavy pause.

My breath catches.

She's actually considering it.

My pulse hammers in my ears. "Mum—"

She doesn't look at me right away. Instead, her gaze drifts around the cafe—the vases lined up by the window, the shelves of ribbons and wrapping paper, the framed photos of past events we've catered to. She exhales softly, and for the first time, I see it—the exhaustion settling into the lines of her face.

"I've been here for over twenty years, Lila," she murmurs. "I've seen children grow up, get married, come back with their own families... I've provided flowers for weddings, funerals, new babies—every milestone, every moment."

She trails off, her fingers pressing lightly against the counter. A sadness flickers in her eyes. "Maybe it's time."

No.

No, no, no.

She smiles, but it's the kind of smile that aches.

"I love this place. I always have. But... I won't be here forever."

My heart stumbles.

I grip the counter, my fingers digging into the wood. "Mum—"

"I'm just saying," she continues gently, setting the letter down like it suddenly feels heavier in her hands. "Maybe it's time we ask ourselves how much more we can fight."

The words hang in the air, pressing in on my ribs, squeezing the breath from my lungs.

I can't speak.

For a second—just a second—I let myself picture it. The cafe without us. The sign coming down. The shop silent, empty, erased.

A future where this place—our place—doesn't belong to us anymore.

Ben Ashcroft gets exactly what he wants.

The thought makes me sick.

I snatch the letter from the counter, crumpling it into my fist.

"No." My voice is firm, steady. Final. "I don't care how much it is. He thinks he can throw crumbs at us and we'll take it? Screw that."

Olivia grins. "There she is."

Sophie shakes her head. "He really thinks he can just buy you out that easily?"

Willow, who's been quiet up until now, frowns. "But why offer this little? If he wants the property, why low ball it?"

I inhale sharply, my anger simmering just beneath the surface. "Because he wants to see if I'll break first."

He's testing me.

Seeing if I'm desperate enough and I hate that he thinks I might be.

Sophie taps her fingers against the counter, thoughtful. "And if you refuse?"

"Then he'll increase the offer."

We all know it.

It's a game to him. He's playing the long con, waiting to see when I'll cave.

Maeve suddenly chimes in, her little voice breaking through the tension. "Are we mad at the coffee man?"

Olivia laughs, reaching over to ruffle her daughter's curls. "Very, very mad."

Maeve gasps dramatically. "Oh no! Should I put him in time-out?"

Sophie snorts into her tea. "Please do."

A reluctant smile tugs at the corner of my lips.

But I don't feel like smiling. Not really.

Because Mum is still looking at the crumpled letter in my hands, the sadness lingering in her expression and for the first time since this all started, I see it—she's tired.

She doesn't want to fight anymore and that?

That pisses me off more than anything.

Ben Ashcroft thinks he can come back after fifteen years and take everything from us? Thinks he can wear us down just enough to make us walk away?

He has no idea who he's dealing with.

I straighten my spine, lifting my chin. "He can take his pathetic offer and shove it."

I glance at my mum. "You deserve more."

Sophie claps her hands together. "Agreed."

Mum sighs, shaking her head at all of us. "At least finish your food before you start declaring war."

"Auntie Mei, I finished my food!" Maeve declares, beaming up at her.

Mum laughs, cupping Maeve's cheek fondly. "Then you're the only one with any sense around here."

Maeve nods proudly and goes back to drawing tulips on her charity cards.

Tulips. The symbol of hope. The flower for Parkinson's awareness.

My gaze drifts back to my mum, to the way she watches us all with quiet warmth, to the way her hands have worn over the years from decades of working this shop.

She thinks we might have to let it go.

That we might lose.

I turn back to the letter, fingers tightening around it.

No.

Not if I have anything to say about it.

Tomorrow, I'm going to march into Ben Ashcroft's office and make it very, very clear.

He might be willing to play dirty.

**But I play to win.**

# 9

# Lila

I storm through the streets, the crumpled letter burning in my grip. The Kingsley Hotel looms ahead—sleek, modern, polished to perfection. Just like him. Just like the life he built after he walked away.

Now he thinks he can waltz back in, throw some money at me, and take the last thing I have left?

I let out a sharp, humourless laugh. No, not today.

I push through the revolving doors with a bit too much force.

His offer was an insult. He was an insult.

The air-conditioning blasts against my heated skin, but it does nothing to cool the fury curling hot and tight inside me. The Kingsley's lobby is too pristine —white marble floors, warm golden lighting, the faint murmur of business deals and expensive champagne being poured.

I shouldn't be here. I should be back at the shop, finishing the bouquets for Sophie's gala.

Fifteen years. The memory hits before I can stop it.

The first time.

*We'd been together for a year. A whole year of Ben being patient, being careful, being a gentleman. Never pushing, always waiting and I loved him for it.*

*His body above mine, his hand tangled in my hair, his lips brushing against my ear as he whispered, "Are you sure?"*

*I was breathless, my heart a frantic drum against my ribs. "Yes."*

*That was all it took.*

*His mouth met mine, hesitant at first, then deepening, a slow, nervous kind of urgency. His hands skimmed my skin. Not confident, not practiced—just careful. Trembling fingers tracing the curve of my waist, like he was scared of getting it wrong.*

*We were both shaking.*

*Tangled in sheets, breathless and unsure, figuring it out together. Heat, nerves, and something deeper—something we didn't have the words for yet.*

*At that moment, the world outside didn't exist. There was only us.*

*Above us, my origami cranes swayed in slow, weightless circles, suspended from the mobile overhead. Caught in the soft current of air, their folded wings cast shifting shadows across the bed, moving with every shaky breath I took. I watched them drift, my chest rising and falling in time with their lazy dance.*

*I remember the way his breath evened out as we lay there, the heat of his body pressed against mine, his fingers trailing absent-mindedly over my bare shoulder. I was sore in a way that made me blush, but I felt safe. Wrapped up in him, warm, drowsy, the steady thrum of his heartbeat beneath my cheek.*

*His hand slid down to my waist, pulling me closer, his lips brushing the top of my head. "You okay?"*

*I nodded against him, my voice a murmur. "Mmm."*

*The room was quiet, only the soft hum of the night filtering through the open window. The world outside still didn't matter.*

*Not yet.*

*Then his phone buzzed.*

*A sharp vibration against the nightstand.*

*Ben groaned, shifting against me. His arm flexed around my waist like he didn't want to move.*

*"Leave it," I murmured, pressing closer, tightening my hold on him.*

*His hesitation lasted a beat, maybe two. Then, with a heavy sigh, he reached for the phone.*

*I caught his wrist, fingers curling around it, guiding it back down to the mattress. "Ben."*

*His eyes met mine in the dim light, searching, uncertain.*

*"Just ignore it," I whispered. "Stay with me."*

*Something flickered in his gaze—something soft, something certain.*

*He exhaled slowly, then switched the phone off, tucking it under the pillow.*

*His arms wound around me again, pulling me flush against him, his lips pressing against my forehead.*

*"Always," he murmured and for the last time, I let myself believe him.*

The memory clings to me like smoke, thick and suffocating.

*Always.*

A promise that shattered the moment reality came knocking. Sophie had offered to come with me, she said to meet me here, but she's late and I don't have the patience for late—every second only fuels the fire clawing deeper in my chest.

Screw it.

I march straight to the reception desk. The woman behind the counter barely glances up from her screen before pasting on a professional smile.

"Hello, I need to see Ben Ashcroft," I say, cutting straight through the polite hum of the room.

Her brows lift slightly. "I'm sorry, miss, but I can't give out guest details."

I exhale through my nose, barely holding on to my patience. "I know he's staying here."

"I'm afraid I can't confirm or deny that."

"Look," I grit out, pressing my palms flat against the counter. "I just need to—"

"Lila!"

I spin just as Sophie rushes in, breathless, her bag nearly slipping off her shoulder. "Sorry, sorry! Traffic was insane." She stops short, scanning my face before glancing at the receptionist, immediately sensing the stand-off. "Is everything okay?"

"She won't let me up," I mutter, throwing a glare toward the woman behind the desk. Sophie straightens, smoothing a hand over her blouse as she flashes a warm, practiced smile—the kind that wins over boardrooms and, more importantly, hotel staff. "I think there's been a little mix-up," she says smoothly, her tone friendly but firm. "Mr Ashcroft is expecting us."

The receptionist hesitates, lips pressing into a thin line.

Sophie leans in slightly, her voice dropping to something conspiratorial. "Come on, Lisa," she says, her smile widening. "Mr Kingsley wouldn't be too happy if he knew you were making his girlfriend wait in the lobby."

The receptionist—Lisa, apparently—lets out a slow breath, her fingers tapping against the keyboard.

"I don't suppose you're asking me this as a guest?" Lisa mutters, already reaching for the spare key card.

Sophie grins. "I'm asking you as someone who will personally make sure you get the best shifts next week."

Lisa sighs, but there's no real fight in it. With a small shake of her head, she pulls a card from the drawer and slides it across the counter. "Penthouse suite."

I snatch it before she can change her mind.

"You're the best, Lisa," Sophie says, winking. "I owe you one."

Lisa rolls her eyes but doesn't protest. The moment we step toward the lift, I press the button for the top floor, gripping the key card tight.

Sophie smirks. "Don't worry about Lisa. She's always been a bit of a battle-axe, but you just have to know how to chip away at her."

The doors slide shut with a soft chime, and the lift hums to life, rising smoothly.

It slows slightly, taking its time between floors, the soft whirring of machinery filling the space. I shift my weight, glancing at Sophie. "Is it supposed to be this slow?"

Sophie clears her throat, suddenly very focused on the floor numbers lighting up above the doors. "Uh, yeah… it's, uh, stopped before."

Something about the way she says it makes me pause. Her face tinges slightly pink, her lips pressing together like she's holding something back.

I narrow my eyes. "Sophie."

"What?"

"You're blushing."

"I am not."

I arch a brow, glancing between her and the slow-moving lift. "It would be a nightmare if this thing stopped."

Sophie lets out a quiet cough, tucking a strand of hair behind her ear. "Depends on who you're stuck with."

That's when it clicks.

"Oh my god." I whirl on her, mouth dropping open. "You—" I gesture vaguely around the lift. "You and Marcus—"

Sophie crosses her arms, trying for nonchalance, but the way she bites back a smirk betrays her. "I don't know what you're talking about."

"Sophie!"

She shrugs, her smirk growing. "What? It has its benefits."

I shake my head, fighting a reluctant grin, "I will never be able to stand in this lift normally again."

She chuckles, winking. "That's what Marcus said too."

As I glance at her, something tugs at my chest—something warm, something bittersweet.

She's happy. Truly, effortlessly happy.

It's written in the way she smiles, the way her eyes light up when she talks about Marcus. She has someone who adores her, who looks at her like she hung the stars, who would probably set the world on fire if she asked. Creating a Foundation to help with Parkinson's in honour of her father and she lets herself have it. I swallow hard, forcing my gaze forward as the lift finally reaches the top floor. I should be happy for her—I am happy for her. But there's a tiny, selfish part of me, a whisper of a thought I don't want to acknowledge, curling in the back of my mind.

She has what I once wanted.

What I used to dream about when I was seventeen and reckless and so stupidly in love with Ben that I thought nothing else in the world mattered.

Now I'm standing in a five-star hotel, preparing to fight for my family's business and livelihood. Sophie nudges me with her elbow, bringing me back. "You okay?"

I blink, exhaling sharply. "Yeah. Just... trying my best not to commit a crime in the next ten minutes."

Sophie hums, tapping her fingers against the lift railing. "That's fair. Just... maybe don't break anything in there?"

I frown. "What, like the furniture?"

"No, the antique duck."

I blink. "The what?"

Sophie sighs, like she's already exhausted by this conversation. "Marcus has this weird, weird attachment to an antique ceramic duck in the penthouse suite. Hand-painted. Imported from France. I don't know. Apparently, it's 'a conversation piece.'"

I stare at her. "And you allow this?"

She deadpans, "Do you think I have any control over that man?"

I let out a short, incredulous laugh, despite the fire still burning in my chest. "I stormed in here ready to verbally eviscerate Ben, and now I'm just picturing some ridiculous bird judging me from the corner of the room."

Sophie smirks. "It does have very judgmental eyes."

I groan, rubbing my temples. "Okay, noted. No duck murder."

Sophie shifts beside me as the lift doors slide open. "Want backup?" Her tone is still light, but there's now a hint of seriousness beneath it.

I hesitate for half a second—just long enough for the idea to tempt me—but then I shake my head. "No. I need to do this myself."

She watches me carefully, then nods. "Alright. But if you don't come back down in an hour, I'm sending a search party. Or a clean-up crew, depending on how this goes."

"If I commit a crime, I trust you to make it look like an accident."

"Obviously." She smirks, stepping back into the lift. "Good luck."

I exhale sharply as I head down the hallway, my fingers tightening around the key card. The weight in my chest creeps back in.

After all this time, I'm finally facing him on my terms. My pulse stutters, my grip faltering.

What if—?

No.

I straighten my spine, shoving the hesitation down.

I cannot let him win.

# 10

## Ben

I know she's coming before she even reaches the door. Lisa at reception calls me, her tone clipped but with a trace of intrigue. "Mr Ashcroft, there's a guest on her way up to see you. She seems... determined."

Lisa has been eyeing me since I checked in—too eager, too interested. The sharp, furious knock comes next.

I smile, rolling my shoulders back, but my pulse is already kicking up. I knew she'd come.

But I didn't expect this heat curling under my skin, this damn anticipation thrumming through my veins.

Another knock—harder this time.

I exhale sharply, then pull open the door and there she is. Flushed, breathing hard, dark eyes burning as she glares up at me. Her hair is wild from the wind, loose strands framing her face, untamed and just as fierce as she is. She shoves past me before I can say a word. The scent of her—jasmine, fresh-cut stems, and the crisp bite of spring rain—flooding my senses.

A crumpled piece of paper smacks against my chest.

I barely catch it before it hits the floor.

"What the hell is this?" she demands, spinning on her heel, arms crossed like she's holding herself together through sheer force of will.

I glance down at the letter I sent her yesterday. I'd expected her to storm in the same day, not leave me stewing overnight. Turns out, she made me wait and I hate waiting. I lean back against the table, folding my arms, watching her. "It's called a buyout offer, sweetheart. Most people read them before storming through hotel suites."

Her nostrils flare. "That's not an offer. It's an insult."

I bite back a smirk. Because she's right. It was low—deliberately so. I knew she'd never take it. That was never the point.

The point was to get her here.

Now she's right where I want her.

She throws her hands up. "You actually think you can waltz back in, throw some money at me, and we just roll over and let you take everything my mother and I have worked for?"

I tilt my head, watching the fire in her eyes, the flush on her cheeks. She's fucking breathtaking when she's angry. "Yes."

Her mouth parts like I just slapped her.

Then she lets out a sharp, humourless laugh.

"Right," she says, shaking her head. "Of course. Because Ben Ashcroft doesn't just buy things. He breaks them first."

That lands.

A muscle ticks in my jaw. I push off the table, closing the space between us. She doesn't back away. I drop my voice. "You think I want to break you?"

Her voice is sharp, but beneath it, there's something else. Something unsteady. She lifts her chin, dark eyes blazing. "Isn't that the plan? Wear us down? Make me beg?"

I exhale sharply, a dark hunger curling low in my gut. *If she's going to beg, it'll be for something much filthier.*

"No?" She tilts her head. Taunting. Daring. "What do you want, then?"

I scramble for logic, for something that makes sense—the cafe. The damn building. Money.

*Her.*

But I don't say that. I can't.

Instead, I hold her gaze, letting the silence stretch. Her eyes search mine, dark and stormy, something unreadable flickering beneath the anger. Then she lets out a quiet, bitter laugh.

"Why now, Ben?" Her voice is steady, but there's something raw beneath it. "Why Nottingham, of all places?"

I keep my expression blank, but my jaw tightens.

She exhales sharply, shaking her head. "We both know why you're back."

Something in the way she says it makes my pulse kick up.

We both know.

Do we?

I open my mouth, but nothing comes out. Because for the first time in years, I don't have the right words.

She steps back, putting space between us, but her eyes never leave mine. "You can pretend this is about business. But we both know that's bullshit."

A muscle ticks in my jaw. "Careful, Lila."

Her eyes flash. "You don't need to hurt other people in the process."

I frown, my head tilting slightly. "What the hell does that mean?"

She doesn't let me interrupt.

"You're not just punishing me—you're threatening the

livelihoods of everyone in that street. You're trying to force us out, and for what? A bigger bottom line?" Her voice cracks slightly. "This is people's lives. Our community." She exhales, quieter now. "You've already made it, Ben. Congratulations—you've done well for yourself." Her eyes linger on mine, softer but still firm. "But you don't need to prove it here."

Her words hit harder than I expect, slipping under the armour I didn't realise I was still wearing.

I grit out, "That's not it."

Her brows lift sharply. "Then what is it, Ben?" Her voice rises, brittle with frustration. "Because from where I'm standing, all I see is a man throwing his weight around just to prove he still can."

"I'm not—" I start, but she cuts me off.

"You don't get to bulldoze your way back into my life and pretend this is about business. You don't get to play puppeteer while the rest of us struggle to stay afloat."

"I'm not trying to control you," I snap, jaw clenched.

"Then what are you trying to do?" she fires back, eyes blazing now. "Punish me? Test me? Remind me that you're the one with all the power now?"

We're toe to toe, the air between us crackling with heat, with resentment, with something so raw it makes my skin prickle. Her voice lowers, trembling with something deeper. "You left, Ben. You walked away. So why are you here trying to destroy the one thing I have left?"

She shoves at my chest, a sharp, frustrated motion. "This is all just a game isn't it?"

Just like that, we're too close. I catch her wrist before she can pull away.

"No," she snaps, trying to yank free. "No—you don't get to

come back and do this. You don't get to tear everything apart and then act like—"

But I don't let her finish.

Something in me snaps.

I grab her, pulling her in, crushing my mouth to hers before she can get another word out.

It's not gentle. It's not careful. It's raw and reckless and years too late.

She gasps, fists slamming into my chest—but she doesn't push me away. Not really. Her hands curl in my shirt instead, like she's fighting herself more than me. Like she's just as furious, just as lost in this as I am.

My arm wraps around her waist, yanking her closer. I kiss her harder—deeper—like I'm trying to burn every second of distance between us.

She tastes like everything I used to want. Everything I still do and when she kisses me back—wild, unfiltered, nails digging into my skin—I know I've already lost whatever control I was clinging to. I slide my hand into her hair, tilting her head to take her deeper, drinking in every sound she makes—every trembling breath, every stifled moan, every trace of the girl I used to know and the woman she's become.

I can't stop.

I don't want to.

I press her back against the door, swallowing every sharp breath, every ragged gasp.

This. This is what I wanted.

Not the cafe. Not the fucking buyout. Her.

She pulls back suddenly, panting, her pupils blown wide and then?

She shoves me—hard.

I stumble back half a step, my own chest heaving. She takes a step back, chest rising and falling too fast, fingers twitching at her sides like she wants to reach for something—steady herself, maybe. But there's nothing to hold on to. Nothing except the one thing she doesn't trust. She drags the back of her hand over her mouth, like she can wipe away the taste of me. Like she needs to and that's when I see it.

She's not just furious at me.

She's furious at herself.

Because she wanted it too.

"What the hell was that?" she breathes, her voice shaking.

I take a slow step forward, hands twitching at my sides, my body still burning with the feel of her. She watches me warily, dark eyes flashing, her breath uneven.

Then she lifts a shaking hand, palm flat like a warning. "You don't get to do that, Ben."

"Don't pretend you didn't want it."

Her eyes flash. "I hate you."

I let out a low, breathless laugh. "Liar."

Her hand balls into a fist. "You are the worst mistake I ever made."

That? That fucking stings.

I open my mouth to fire back, but she's already yanking open the door.

"I mean it," she says, voice hoarse. "Don't come near me again."

The door slams. The sound echoes through the suite, rattling through my chest.

I stand there, breathing hard, fingers curled into fists.

The taste of her is still on my lips. The heat of her body still lingers against mine, seared into my skin like a brand I can't scrub off.

I knew I shouldn't have done it—I knew the second my mouth crashed against hers that I was making a mistake.

But I couldn't stop.

I don't stop when it comes to Lila. That's the problem. That's always been the problem.

Now she's gone, her final words slamming into my chest.

*Don't come near me again.*

I drag a hand through my hair, exhaling sharply, and push away from the door. The room feels too big, too empty. I stalk toward the minibar, yanking open the cabinet and grabbing the first bottle I see. Vodka.

Perfect.

I pour a measure, no ice, no thought—just knock it back in one go. The burn barely registers. I pour another.

Fine. Screw it.

If this is what she wants—distance, silence, goodbye—then so be it.

I could have anyone. Hell, I could walk downstairs right now and find someone willing to warm my bed before the night's out. No names. No complications. Just skin and distraction.

I don't need her.

I don't—

The lie crumbles halfway through the second swallow.

Because even as I try to picture it—anyone else—her face cuts through. Her voice, sharp and bright. The fire in her eyes. The way her hands trembled against my chest when I kissed her, not just from anger—but from want.

Suddenly it's laughable. This pretence. This idea that

someone else could ever come close.

Because it's always been her.

I fucked up.

I'd spent years imagining what it would be like to see her again. What I'd say. How I'd play it. Cool, controlled, untouchable—because that's who I am now. The version of me that doesn't break, doesn't chase, doesn't lose.

But then she walked in, eyes blazing, tearing into me like no one else ever has, and it all unravelled.

I'd spent years trying to bury her and one kiss was all it took to prove that I never really had. I pace toward the window, my pulse still thrumming like I just stepped out of a fight. Because that's what it was, wasn't it?

A fight and I kissed her in the middle of it.

No finesse, no calculated moves—just a pure, reckless need.

Fucking idiot.

I rake a hand through my hair, jaw tight. I should've handled it differently. The low ball offer was a mistake—I see that now. I'd justified it to myself, convinced it was the only way to get her in a room alone. Because if I'd gone in too high, she'd have been suspicious. She'd have known I was playing a different game.

But instead of reeling her in, I pushed her away. Hard and now she hates me even more than she already did.

I let out a bitter laugh, shaking my head. I should let it go. Walk away, cut my losses.

But I don't want to let it go.

She kissed me back.

For a second—just a second—she melted into me, her fingers gripping my shirt like she needed me just as badly as I needed her.

I close my eyes, replaying it. The way she tasted. The way she gasped into my mouth. The way her breath hitched just before she shoved me away.

I know that sound.

It wasn't just anger. It was fear.

Not of me.

Of herself.

That changes everything. Lila might hate me right now. But hate is just love wearing sharper teeth.

I can work with that. I have to.

# 11

## Lila

The charity gala. Sophie's dad. My mum. Our shop. These are the things I should be thinking about.

Not Ben. Not his hands. Not his mouth. Not the fact that even now, I can still feel him on me, days later.

I shake the thought loose, exhaling hard as I move through the grand ballroom of the Kingsley Hotel, the scent of fresh roses, eucalyptus, and candle wax wrapping around me.

The charity fundraiser is in full swing—guests in sleek evening wear sipping champagne, laughter and polite conversation humming beneath the soft melody of the string quartet. The event is perfect. Every table adorned with carefully arranged bouquets, every flower placed with intention, with meaning.

My work.

I should be proud. I should be soaking it in—the elegance, the success, the way Sophie's father lights up when guests approach him, shaking his hand, telling him how important this cause is.

Instead, I'm hiding in plain sight.

Keeping myself busy, flitting from table to table, adjusting stems that don't need adjusting, making sure the hydrangeas aren't drinking up too much water.

Because if I stop—if I stand still for even a second—I might actually have to deal with the fact that I kissed Ben Ashcroft.

That I let myself want him.

Again.

A champagne flute appears in front of me. "You look like you need this."

I glance up. Sophie.

Her gaze is sharp, amused, far too perceptive for my liking.

"I'm fine," I say quickly. "Just making sure everything looks perfect."

She tilts her head, unconvinced. "Lila, the event is stunning. The flowers are stunning. You look stunning. However, you also look like you might start arranging cutlery next if someone doesn't stop you."

I sigh, taking the glass. "I just need to stay busy."

Sophie hums. "Right and this has absolutely nothing to do with Ben?"

I nearly choke on my drink.

"I—"

She lifts a hand. "Don't even try. I saw the way you practically bolted out of the Kingsley yesterday. One second you were storming in, ready to commit murder—next thing I know, you're gone without a trace. Her eyes narrow, sharp with suspicion. "You know him, don't you?"

I freeze for a split second—too long. Sophie's gaze sharpens, locking in like a predator sensing weakness. Willow appears beside her like some kind of interrogation backup, her eyes glint, victorious. "I knew it."

I exhale sharply, dragging a hand through my hair. "It's... complicated."

Sophie's lips curve into a slow, knowing smirk. "Complicated?" she echoes, drawing out the word like she's savouring it. "Lila, you don't do complicated."

"That's exactly why this is a problem," I mutter.

Willow grins. "Tell me this doesn't sound like something straight out of a novel."

I throw my hands up. "Not at all!"

Willow ignores me, already counting on her fingers. "Angsty backstory? Check. Unresolved tension? Check. A heated confrontation in a penthouse suite?"

Sophie's eyes sparkle. "Did you fight in the suite? Was there yelling? Oh my God, was there a desk involved?"

I groan. "Stop."

But a tiny, traitorous part of me wishes it was just a book. Wishes it came with a guaranteed happy ending, where things would miraculously fall into place. Meeting these women through the book club has been a blessing, a lifeline I didn't know I needed. Their friendships have made the long hours, the stress, the uncertainty easier to bear. But the sad truth is the past doesn't come back to fix things. It comes back to wreck everything all over again. In real life, the man who once promised me always is now the one holding the power to take it all away.

This isn't some neatly plotted romance. It's my life and right now? It's a goddamn mess. Sophie's still watching me, her amusement fading into something softer. "Lila," she says carefully, "what really happened?"

Before I can answer, Olivia rushes in, slightly breathless, Maeve in tow.

"Sorry, sorry! We had a juice-related incident," Olivia announces, adjusting Maeve's dress. "We were almost on time and then someone—" she gives Maeve a pointed look, "—spilled juice all over her dress and of course, only this dress would do."

Maeve crosses her arms, standing her ground. "It's my fancy dress."

Sophie, clearly enjoying the distraction, crouches to Maeve's level. "Well, it is very fancy."

Maeve beams. "I know."

Willow shakes her head, laughing. "This kid's confidence could rule the world."

Olivia sighs. "She knows it."

The tension in my chest eases just slightly. This—the laughter, the teasing, the warmth between us—is exactly what I needed. This night isn't about Ben. It's about Sophie's dad. It's about the community, the people we love, the reason we all came together to make this happen.

I nod toward the entrance. "Come on. We have a fundraiser to run."

Sophie watches me for a second longer, clearly not done with prying, but she lets it go—for now.

But something tells me she won't let me escape for long.

\*\*\*\*\*\*\*\*

I stand near the edge of the ballroom, watching Marcus as he kneels beside Maeve, who's perched on a velvet settee like a tiny queen. Her curls bounce as she giggles, clutching a half-eaten cookie.

Marcus holds up a finger, his tone mock-serious. "Now, Miss

Maeve, you promised me one dance later."

Maeve's eyes light up, and she nods vigorously. "But you have to spin me."

Marcus grins, ruffling her hair. "Deal. The best spins for the best little princess."

I can't help but smile as I watch him, his attention completely focused on Maeve. Then he stands, lifting her up effortlessly and settling her against his hip as he turns to Sophie.

The way they look at each other... God, it's like they're the only two people in the room. Sophie's gaze softens as she reaches out to touch Maeve's cheek, her hand lingering on Marcus's arm.

Maeve leans in, whispering loudly enough for everyone to hear, "Uncle Marcus, you're my favourite."

Marcus chuckles. "Good. Let's keep it that way, kiddo."

Maeve beams, soaking in the attention, her small hands resting on Marcus's shoulders as he holds her securely. My eyes flick back to Marcus, who's now spinning Maeve around like they're dancing, the little girl's laughter ringing out, bright and unrestrained.

Olivia exhales a small, wistful breath. "He's amazing with her," she murmurs, but there's something in the way she says it—something quiet, almost careful.

I glance at her, catching the way her fingers toy with the hem of her sleeve, the way her smile doesn't quite reach her eyes.

Her eyes stay fixed on Maeve, but her voice drops, quieter now. "If only her dad would just spend five minutes with her."

She exhales sharply, like the weight of those words has been pressing on her for too long. "That's all it would take, you know? Five minutes." Her voice wavers, barely above a whisper. "If he'd just spend some time with her—he'd see how amazing she is. How she has this big, open heart that only knows how to love."

She swipes a hand over her face, as if trying to push the thought away. "But he won't. She'll keep growing, keep loving and he'll never know what he's missing."

I reach for her hand, squeezing it gently. "She has you, Olivia."

She swallows, her gaze still locked on her daughter. "I know." A small, sad smile flickers across her lips. "I just hope that's enough."

I hesitate for half a second. Olivia isn't the type to show cracks in her armour—she's the one who always has a plan, always pushes forward, always knows what to do. Seeing her like this, raw and uncertain, makes my chest ache.

I slide an arm around her shoulders and pull her in. She stiffens at first, like she's not used to being the one comforted, but then she exhales, sinking into the hug.

For a moment, she stays still, her breath a little uneven against my shoulder. Then, so softly I almost miss it, she murmurs, "Thank you."

I squeeze her a little tighter. "Always."

Marcus's phone buzzes. He shifts Maeve to his hip, frowning slightly as he glances at the screen. He smoothly shifts Maeve into Sophie's arms as he takes the call.

"Excuse me a second."

Sophie's brows furrow as she watches him walk a few steps away, the easy smile slipping from her face. "Is everything okay?"

Willow shrugs, keeping Maeve entertained with silly faces. "Maybe it's one of his big-shot friends."

Marcus returns a moment later, his expression tight. "So,

minor hiccup," he says, trying for casual but clearly failing. "Our final auction item just fell through."

"What?" Sophie's eyes widen. "Which one?"

"Dr Patterson," Marcus sighs. "He's caught up at the hospital. He was supposed to offer an evening of his company—brainy science stuff, you know? He was a big draw."

Panic ripples through our little group. The auction is a key part of the fundraiser, and a last-minute cancellation is a logistical nightmare.

"Okay," Sophie breathes, tapping her temple as if conjuring ideas. "We need a replacement. Fast."

"Someone interesting," Willow adds, bouncing Maeve slightly on her hip. "Someone people would actually pay to spend an evening with."

The three of them turn to me in unison.

I blink. "What?"

Willow's eyes light up. "Lila, you could do it!"

I stare at her like she's just sprouted a second head. "Me? Why would anyone bid to spend an evening with me?"

Sophie rolls her eyes. "Oh, please. You're charming, you're talented, and you run one of the most beloved businesses in the community. You're perfect."

"You can offer something unique," Olivia adds, her excitement growing. "Like an evening baking lesson. Or a private flower arrangement class. People would love that!"

I open my mouth to argue, but Willow steps in, nodding firmly. "She's right. It's a great idea."

"But—"

Maeve bounces in Willow's arms, eyes wide. "I'd bid for cookies!"

I can't help the small laugh that escapes me, despite the

lingering nerves. "You'd be my only customer, Maeve."

Marcus sets a hand on my shoulder, his expression warm and sincere. "Seriously, Lila. You'd be helping us out."

I hesitate, my heart pounding. But as I look around the room—at Sophie, at Marcus. This is a great cause, something that is close to their hearts—I know I can't say no.

"Fine," I say, exhaling sharply. "But don't blame me if it's a flop."

Sophie claps her hands together, her grin wide and bright. "It's going to be amazing. I can feel it."

"Great," I mutter, crossing my arms. "Now I just have to hope some poor soul wants to spend an evening with me."

Sophie grins, hooking her arm through mine. "Trust me, Lila. This is going to be the highlight of the night."

God, I hope not.

# 12

## Lila

This was a terrible idea. I knew it when Sophie grabbed my hand and practically shoved me onto the stage, beaming like this was the most brilliant thing ever.

Standing under the intense spotlight, an entire ballroom watching me, my stomach is absolutely in my throat.

The auctioneer smiles at me, oblivious to my discomfort. "For our next auction item, we have something truly special."

From the side of the stage, Sophie is grinning like an idiot, giving me an overly enthusiastic thumbs-up. Like this is fun. Like I'm not seconds away from spontaneous combustion.

I glare at her. She winks. She's not about to be bid on like some charity dating show gone wrong. I plaster on a polite smile, hands clasped in front of me, ignoring the amused murmurs rippling through the crowd. Sophie had pitched this as a fun experience, an evening of baking and floral arranging, but the moment I stepped onto the stage, it became abundantly clear that some of the attendees—particularly the older men at the front tables—thought they were bidding on me, not a workshop.

I swear one of them just adjusted his glasses for a better look. God, kill me now.

I clear my throat as the auctioneer continues. "A private, hands-on baking and floral arrangement class with Lila Ng, owner of Bloom & Brew. A unique experience that combines art, food, and creativity!"

A smattering of applause. Some nods of interest. I force my shoulders to stay loose, even though my pulse is sprinting.

"It's a wonderful opportunity to learn from a beloved member of our community," the auctioneer adds. "Shall we start the bidding at fifty pounds?"

A polite bid comes from an older woman near the back. Thank God.

"Fifty pounds," the auctioneer announces. "Do I hear seventy-five?"

Another hand goes up. Then another. A slow but steady pace.

Okay. Okay. This isn't so bad.

Then a smooth, deep voice cuts through the chatter.

"Ten thousand pounds."

I freeze.

The auctioneer blinks. The entire ballroom stills.

Sophie's jaw drops. Olivia chokes on her champagne. Willow lets out a strangled noise that sounds suspiciously like a squeal.

I don't even need to turn around to know exactly who it is.

Ben.

Of course.

He's draped in his chair like he has nowhere better to be, the crisp black tux fitting him too damn well, the open collar just undone enough to hint at something reckless beneath the polish. His dark blond hair is slicked back, like he ran his fingers through it just to mess it up. One wrist rests lazily on the edge of his chair, fingers tapping idly against the table, like he has all the time in the world. Like he owns the damn place.

His gaze is locked on mine, unreadable, waiting.

The auctioneer visibly chokes. "Ah—well—that's—" He coughs, straightening his bow tie, eyes darting toward the crowd like he needs confirmation that he didn't just hallucinate that number. "We have a bid of ten thousand pounds."

The auctioneer clears his throat again, visibly rattled. "Do I hear eleven thousand?"

Crickets.

Not a single hand raises. No one even breathes.

Of course not. Who the hell is going to bid against that?

I force my jaw to unclench, but my heart is still hammering so loud I swear the microphone might pick it up.

"Going once," the auctioneer says, hesitating for half a second, like maybe someone will swoop in and save me from whatever the hell Ben thinks he's doing.

No one does.

"Going twice."

I swallow hard.

"Sold! To bidder number—" The auctioneer scans the crowd, brow furrowing. "Sir, if you could hold up your number, please?"

Slowly, deliberately, Ben raises his number card, the movement so effortlessly smug it makes my blood boil. The auctioneer barely finishes confirming, "Bidder number seventy-two!" The room erupts with applause, a wave of claps and murmured excitement rippling through the ballroom, but I barely hear it over the blood roaring in my ears.

Ben doesn't look at the auctioneer. His gaze stays locked on mine, dark blond hair slicked back, a hint of stubble sharpening his jawline. He looks infuriatingly good—like the kind of man who knows he just turned the entire night in his favour.

The worst part?

He has the audacity to smirk.

Ben just lifts his glass toward me in a silent toast.

Smug. Smug. Smug.

I am going to murder him.

******

I grip the edge of the podium so hard my knuckles ache, my stomach still flipping like I'm in free fall.

Ten thousand pounds.

For an evening with me.

Or at least, that's what the entire room is whispering about. Never mind that it's supposed to be a workshop—a business experience. No. Ben Ashcroft had to go and make it look like I was some sort of high-priced date.

The bastard.

The second the auctioneer moves on to the next item, Sophie tugs me off the stage, her grip like a vice. "What. The. Hell?" she whisper-yells, dragging me to the side of the ballroom.

"I don't know!" I hiss back. "You think I planned for that?"

She whirls toward Willow and Olivia, who are already waiting, eyes wide, half in shock, half in pure, unfiltered amusement. Olivia shakes her head. "That was the single most unhinged power move I have ever seen."

Willow exhales slowly, adjusting her dress. "It was kind of hot, though."

I shoot her a glare.

Sophie folds her arms, glancing back toward Ben. "Well, if his goal was to make an entire room think you two have unresolved sexual tension, then congratulations, mission accomplished."

My stomach twists.

Because we do have unresolved tension and now it's a ten-thousand-pound disaster.

I open my mouth to respond when a deep, amused voice cuts in.

"So."

We all turn.

Marcus. Looking every inch the intimidating businessman in his tux, sipping his whiskey with the cool, calculating gaze of a man who's just been handed a puzzle he intends to solve.

That puzzle?

Ben Ashcroft.

"Where's your admirer?" Marcus muses, cocking a brow.

"He's not my admirer," I grit out.

Marcus tilts his head. "No? He just dropped ten grand for a casual night of flower arranging?"

Willow hums. "Maybe he's really passionate about floral design."

I groan, pressing my fingers to my temple. "Will you all stop?"

Marcus doesn't. He just studies me like I'm a contract he's about to renegotiate. "So. You okay with this?"

The question is careful, but there's a quiet steel beneath it. He's watching for any hesitation, any sign that I'm not okay with it.

Honestly, I don't know what I am, but Ben has offered to donate a considerable amount for their cause.

I cross my arms, forcing my voice steady. "I can handle Ben."

Marcus looks unconvinced. "You sure?"

Sophie nudges him with her elbow. "Marcus, relax. If Ben tries anything, Lila will rip him apart before you even get the chance."

His lips press into a thin line, then he looks back at me, unreadable. "Lila, you don't have to go through with this," he says, voice steady, measured. "If you don't want to do it, I'll cover the donation. Ten grand, twenty—doesn't matter. You're not stuck."

The words hit somewhere deep, unexpected. Not just because Marcus offering to casually drop a fortune on me is something I never saw coming, but because… he means it. There's no expectation, no hidden agenda—just the quiet, solid reassurance that I have an out if I need it.

Marcus might be a billionaire, but he's also fiercely loyal. Protective in a way that isn't possessive—just steady, unwavering. The kind of person who would go to war for the people he cares about without hesitation.

Sophie caught a good one. A frigging unicorn that you only read about in books.

I swallow hard. "It's fine," I say, softer this time. "Really."

His sharp gaze flickers over me, assessing, searching, but I hold steady.

Sophie steps closer, resting a hand on Marcus's chest in that effortless way she always does—like she's the only one who can tame the storm brewing beneath his sharp exterior. "Babe," she murmurs, her voice soft but firm. "Let Lila handle it."

Sophie turns to me, her expression gentler now. "Are you sure, Lila? You don't have to do this. This was supposed to be fun, and if it's not—" She squeezes my arm. "We can figure something out."

There it is. The escape hatch. A way out, if I want it.

I swallow, something warm curling in my chest at her concern. "I'm sure."

Sophie searches my face for another second before nodding. Then she smiles, something full of quiet gratitude. "Thank you," she says sincerely. "This is an incredible thing you're doing."

Beside her, Marcus exhales sharply, reluctant but relenting. "Alright." His voice is measured, controlled. But then his eyes harden slightly. "Just know—if he so much as looks at you the wrong way, I'll handle it."

Sophie rolls her eyes, but there's a hint of amusement in her exasperation. "You're very intimidating, babe. We all appreciate it."

Before Marcus can double down on his threat, a tiny voice pipes up from behind him.

"Who are you handling?"

Maeve tugs at the hem of her mum's dress, her big eyes blinking up at all of us, clearly unimpressed that something interesting is happening without her.

Olivia smothers a laugh. "No one, sweetheart. Uncle Marcus is just being dramatic."

Marcus makes a noise of protest, but before he can defend himself, Maeve turns her attention to me, then to Ben across the room. She squints at him, tilting her head like she's studying a strange bug under a microscope. "Is he the coffee man?"

I sigh. "Yes, Maeve. He's the coffee man."

She purses her lips, nodding sagely, then leans in close—conspiratorial. "He's too handsome—I don't trust him."

Willow chokes on a laugh, and Olivia looks like she's never been prouder. Marcus grins, ruffling Maeve's hair. "Smart kid."

Maeve puffs up like she's just been awarded a medal. Then she narrows her eyes across the ballroom. "Maybe I should put him in time-out."

Sophie loses it, laughing into Marcus's shoulder, and Olivia wipes at her eyes like she's overwhelmed by her daughter's brilliance.

I can't help it—I laugh too. Because, honestly? She's not wrong.

Maeve gives one last suspicious glance at Ben before trotting off in search of more desserts, satisfied that she's delivered justice.

Marcus sighs, shaking his head. "I like her. She's got good instincts."

Sophie pats his chest. "Yes, babe. But you can't put Ben Ashcroft in time-out."

Marcus mutters something about that being debatable, but I'm still laughing, and for the first time all night, the tightness in my chest eases.

Too bad it won't last.

Because when I glance back across the ballroom, Ben's standing. Drink in hand, expression unreadable, as he starts making his way toward us.

Straight towards me.

# 13

## Ben

The second I made that bid, I felt the shift.

Not from Lila—I expected her to be pissed—but from the collective force of her inner circle.

Now I'm walking straight into enemy territory.

Sophie. Willow. Olivia. They close ranks the moment I step closer, forming a human shield around Lila like she needs protecting from me. Their expressions vary—Olivia's is sharp, unreadable, Sophie's assessing, Willow's unimpressed—but the underlying message is the same:

You're not welcome here.

Yet, here I am.

I take a slow sip of my whiskey, letting them look their fill.

I've already done my homework on them.

Had Shaw dig up everything in Lila's world.

Sophie Parkes—corporate strategist at Kingsley Global Strategies, engaged to Marcus Kingsley.

Willow Rivera—librarian. Runs Silverbeck Library.

Olivia Harper—HR director at Iron Link Engineering. Single mother to four-year-old Maeve.

## BEN

They all met through Sophie's book club—Books That Bang.

I nearly choked on my whiskey when I read the report.

Lila reads smut.

Not just romance—filthy books. A slow smirk tugs at my lips. Yeah. That tracks.

Now I can't stop picturing it—Lila curled up in bed, eyes skimming over something indecent, cheeks flushed, breath catching.

Jesus.

I take another slow sip of my whiskey, forcing my focus back on the present—on the three women currently sizing me up like they're debating whether to tear me apart now or let Lila finish the job later.

Get your shit together, Ashcroft.

Because right now? They look like they want to lynch me.

Lila's standing just behind them, arms folded so tight it's a wonder she hasn't cut off circulation. Her glare is pure murder.

Good. I'd be disappointed if she wasn't still pissed.

I consider my options.

Rising to the fight would be easy. Giving them attitude, matching their energy. But that's what Lila expects. She wants me to be the arrogant, insufferable bastard she's built up in her head.

So, naturally, I decide to do the one thing guaranteed to really piss her off.

I turn on the charm.

A slow, easy smile. Relaxed shoulders. The picture of calm, effortless amusement. Like I haven't just walked into the lion's den.

Like I belong here.

Sophie tilts her head, unimpressed. "You must be Ben

Ashcroft. The man who just spent ten thousand pounds on an evening with our Lila."

I raise my glass slightly. "Worth every penny."

Lila gives me a saccharine smile, all teeth. "It's non-refundable."

Then, before Sophie can sharpen that unimpressed look into a full-blown verbal evisceration, I glance around the ballroom and let my expression soften—just enough.

"You've done something incredible here," I say, my voice smooth but sincere. "The turnout, the fundraising, the cause itself—it's impressive. You should be proud."

That catches her off guard. Just for a second.

Marcus, standing beside her, watches me carefully, his expression unreadable. Sophie tilts her head, lips pressing together, considering me like she's trying to decide if I'm actually being genuine or just laying the groundwork for whatever game she thinks I'm playing.

The truth?

I mean it.

I might be here for Lila, but I can respect what they've done. The fundraiser isn't just another glitzy event for rich people to pat themselves on the back—it actually matters. The energy in the room, the way the whole community is truly invested in raising money, the way Sophie's father is being treated like a person and not just the face of the cause... it's impressive.

Sophie studies me for a beat longer, her sharp gaze assessing. Then, just as I think she might push back again, she exhales, a small, genuine smile breaking through. "Thank you," she says, her voice softer this time. "It's a very generous donation—we appreciate it."

"So, Ben," Olivia says, arms crossed, gaze assessing. "You're a businessman. Surely, ten grand is pocket change to you."

I shrug, taking another slow sip of whiskey. "Depends on what I'm buying."

Willow narrows her eyes. "And what exactly do you think you're buying?"

I meet her stare evenly. "An evening of baking and floral arrangements, obviously."

Willow doesn't blink. "Is that's all you're expecting?"

Her tone is casual, but there's an edge beneath it—a quiet warning wrapped in politeness. A test.

I keep my expression easy, letting the moment stretch just long enough to make them wonder. "Unless Lila's planning to throw in a bonus round of business strategy consulting, then yes. That's all I'm expecting."

Sophie hums. "Because if you think you're getting anything else, I assure you—"

Olivia finishes for her, "—you're not."

I exhale through my nose, amused. "Duly noted."

Lila retorts. "These are going to be the most expensive rock cakes you've ever made."

Willow chimes. "Or suffered through."

I smirk, shifting my weight lazily. "Rock cakes? That's what you're planning to make?"

"Depends," she fires back. "Do you prefer them dry and inedible, or just mildly disappointing?"

I let my smirk deepen, tilting my head. "I was thinking iced fingers…" Lila freezes for half a second—barely noticeable, but I catch it. The way her throat moves as she swallows. The flicker of something behind her eyes.

She recovers. She tilts her head, expression flat. "I was thinking more along the lines of a plain digestive."

I arch a brow, fighting back a grin. "Come on, Lila. Not even a ginger nut?"

Her expression doesn't waver. "Nope. Digestive. No chocolate. No caramel. Just dry. Bland. Functional."

Willow winces. "Brutal."

I chuckle, low and amused. "Guess I'll just have to make the best of it."

Lila lifts her chin. "You do that."

But before Lila can fire back, Marcus' voice cuts through the air.

"Ashcroft."

I turn, finding him watching me with that unreadable businessman's stare.

"We need to finalise your donation," he says smoothly, though we both know that's not why he's here.

I exhale slowly, setting my whiskey down. "Of course. Excuse us ladies, wouldn't want any paperwork issues, would we?"

I adjust my cuffs.

We step into a quieter room across the hallway. The energy shifts instantly. Marcus doesn't waste time with pleasantries. He moves with quiet precision, lifting a heavy crystal decanter and pouring a generous measure of Macallan 25, the deep amber liquid catching the low light. He slides it across the counter without a word. I take the glass. Old-school. Serious. The kind of whisky you don't just drink—you respect. Clearly Marcus does, the man knows his whisky.

"That's a sizeable donation," he muses, his tone casual. Too casual. He picks up his own glass, swirling the amber liquid once before taking a slow sip. "Generous." A pause. "But I'm not impressed."

I take the glass, letting the weight of it settle in my palm.

## BEN

"Didn't do it to impress you."

Marcus exhales through his nose, unimpressed. "No, I imagine not." He sets his drink down with deliberate ease, then turns his full attention on me. "You might be used to throwing money around for whatever you want," he says smoothly, "but Lila isn't some escort you can buy for an evening."

The words land like a slap. My grip tightens around the glass, a sharp heat flaring in my chest.

"I never have," I bite out, my voice low and edged with warning. "I never will."

Marcus tilts his head slightly, studying me like he's testing for cracks. "Good," he says, taking another sip of his drink.

He takes a step closer, his voice low, measured. "You screw with her. I dismantle you. Simple."

I take a sip slowly, unfazed. "Sounds expensive."

His gaze hardens. "I can afford it."

The silence stretches, taut and unyielding. Neither of us moves.

I'm pissed.

"You don't know a damn thing about me, Kingsley."

Marcus lifts his glass, his gaze steady, unreadable. "I know enough. You left. You're back and now, for whatever reason, you've decided Lila is your business again." He sets the glass down with deliberate precision, his voice cool, controlled. "So let me make something clear—hurt her, and you deal with me."

I take a sip of my whiskey, watching him carefully. "You always this protective over your fiancée's friends?"

He doesn't flinch. "When they're as important to Sophie as Lila is? Yes."

Something sharp twists in my chest.

Marcus isn't here for threats or bravado. He's here because

he cares. Because Lila matters to Sophie, and that means she matters to him. That's what Lila's always deserved. Someone who doesn't leave. I shove the thought aside before it can take root.

For a split second, something tightens in my chest. Protective is one thing—but this? The sheer intensity of it?

However, a flush of something ridiculous creeps in before I shove it down.

Marcus tilts his head slightly, like he's clocked the moment of hesitation. "Relax, Ashcroft. Sophie is the only woman for me."

I exhale slowly, forcing a smirk of my own. "Never thought otherwise."

Marcus doesn't say anything—just gives me one last, sharp look before draining his drink and stepping back.

I hold his stare, the tension between us taut, charged.

"I'm not here to hurt her," I say finally, my voice steady. Certain.

Marcus exhales slowly, tilting his head, considering. Then, with an almost imperceptible shift, he leans back slightly, his grip loosening around his glass—but not before I catch the lingering edge in his expression.

"Then maybe you should start proving it."


'

# 14

## Lila

I haven't slept.

Not really.

I spent half the night tossing and turning, my brain a relentless loop of irritation, frustration, and the lingering memory of his mouth on mine. My pillow smells like roses and espresso—a cruel combination that reminds me too much of the way Ben Ashcroft upended my entire life with one stupid, reckless kiss.

The other half of the night?

Trying to figure out what the hell I'm supposed to bake with him.

Rock cakes were a tempting choice—I could adjust the recipe to make it enough to make him choke, but not quite enough to land me in legal trouble. A wreath crossed my mind at some ungodly hour. Fitting, considering I'm essentially walking into my own funeral later tonight. Maybe I should make him arrange one himself—something classy, with "May you rot in hell" spelled out in carnations.

A dark chuckle escapes me as I sip my now-cold coffee. Sleep deprivation is making me unhinged.

I drag a hand through my hair and glance at the clock. 5:47 a.m.

Fantastic.

Another restless night, another day of trying not to lose my mind before my "Evening of Baking and Floral Arrangements" with the man who kissed me senseless and then had the audacity to bid ten thousand pounds for another chance to torture me.

I need fresh air.

Slipping into leggings, a hoodie, and my most battered trainers, I step out of my flat and head toward the park.

The crisp morning air smacks me in the face. I stuff my hands into my pockets, shoulders hunched against the early chill, and start walking.

The park is almost deserted, save for the sadists pounding the pavement like they actually enjoy running at this ungodly hour.

I watch them pass, their faces twisted in varying degrees of pain, and shake my head. Why? Just... why?

Voluntarily waking up before dawn to be miserable? That's not fitness. That's masochism.

I step off the path, heading toward the quieter part of the park, where the old oak trees line the pond and the world feels a little less suffocating.

That's when I see him.

He's jogging toward me, dressed in loose black joggers and a sweat-damp shirt clinging to his chest, hair tousled by the wind. It's annoyingly unfair—how even mid-run, flushed and breathless, he still looks like trouble wrapped in temptation. Those joggers? Definitely doing things they shouldn't.

God. I hate him.

I consider turning around, pretending I didn't see him. I could blend into the trees. Become one with the ducks. Reclaim my anonymity.

But he spots me first. Slows to a walk and smirks. Because of course he does.

"Well, well," he drawls, wiping his brow with the hem of his shirt—just enough to flash a hint of toned stomach. "Didn't take you for an early riser, Lila."

I scowl. "Didn't take you for a runner. You strike me more as the kind of guy who pays someone to do cardio for him."

His grin is wicked. "Tempting. But some things are better when you do them yourself."

He pauses, eyes flicking over me. "Though, I've heard cardio's a lot more fun with a partner."

He winks. "Keeps the stamina up."

My face lights up like a furnace.

Nope. Absolutely not entertaining that thought.

I clear my throat, folding my arms and throwing him a glare. "What are you even doing here?"

"Running," he says innocently, like it's the most obvious thing in the world.

I shoot him a deadpan look. "Yes, I gathered. But here? In my park?"

He raises an eyebrow. "Your park?"

"You know what I mean."

He steps closer, gaze flicking over me. "What about you? Couldn't sleep?"

I hate that he knows me well enough to guess.

"Not your business," I mutter, shifting my weight. "I just needed fresh air before—"

I stop myself before the words slip.

Before I remind him that later tonight, I have to endure an evening of forced domesticity with him.

His smirk deepens. "Before our date?"

I choke. "It's not a date."

Ben tilts his head, feigning innocence. "I don't know, Lila. There's baking. Flowers. Maybe a candle or two."

"Oh, go to hell."

He grins, slow and lazy. "Already there, sweetheart."

I groan, pressing my fingers to my temples. Why, out of all the people in this damn city, did I have to bump into him?

Ben steps a little closer, lowering his voice. "You don't have to look so miserable about it. You might actually have fun."

I scoff. "I'd rather arrange my own funeral flowers."

Ben laughs, a deep, genuine sound that rumbles through the quiet morning air. Not the sharp-edged amusement he usually throws my way—but real, unguarded.

Something in my chest tightens.

It's been a long time since I've seen him like this.

Not since before.

Not since everything fell apart fifteen years ago.

I shove the thought away before it can take root, but the damage is done. The past seeps in like smoke, curling around my ribs, thick and suffocating.

I shouldn't be noticing this.

Shouldn't be noticing the way his face softens when he laughs, the way his eyes crinkle at the corners, the way—for just a moment—he doesn't look like Ben Ashcroft, a ruthless businessman and my personal tormentor.

He just looks like the boy I used to know.

The boy I lost.

I grit my teeth, shaking off the thought. That boy is gone.

Ben exhales, still grinning, and tilts his head at me. "You always did have a morbid sense of humour."

I force a smirk, masking the sudden ache behind my ribs. "Yet, you paid ten grand to spend an evening with me. Who's the real masochist here?"

His smirk returns, slower this time. "Oh, sweetheart, I never claimed to be anything else."

Damn him.

Damn him and that voice and that look and the way he always—always—knows how to pull me back into this maddening game.

I open my mouth—probably to insult him again—but a gust of wind cuts through the morning air, making me shiver.

Before I can step back, he reaches out and tugs the edge of my hoodie up, flipping the hood over my head. The movement is so smooth, so unthinking, it knocks the breath out of me for a second.

His hands drop away, but his eyes linger, something unreadable flickering beneath the usual arrogance.

It's an old habit.

A remnant of a time when he knew me. I hate how that makes my chest tighten.

The moment stretches, heavier than it should be, and suddenly I feel too seen. Too exposed.

I need to go.

"Enjoy your run, Ashcroft," I say, voice brisk, already stepping back.

"Walk with me?"

It's not a command. Not a challenge.

Just that—a request.

Soft. Almost careful.

I should say no. I should turn on my heel, go home, bury myself in work, and pretend this moment never happened.

But instead, I hesitate. Ben sees it. He exhales, just barely. "Please."

It's quiet. Almost like he doesn't want to say it—but he does.

Like for the first time since he came back, he's asking instead of taking.

That throws me and against my better judgment?

I do.

We walk in silence at first.

The morning air is crisp, the city still rubbing the sleep from its eyes. A few early risers pass us—dog walkers, runners, people who have their lives together enough to function before sunrise.

I am not one of them.

Ben moves with that effortless confidence, like he owns the damn pavement. His hands are tucked into his pockets, his long strides forcing me to keep pace.

It's infuriating how easily he settles into this, like we've done it a hundred times before.

Which, of course, we have.

I shove my hands deeper into my hoodie, scanning the park ahead. The path curves toward the high street, toward places we used to haunt as teenagers—cheap diners, late-night corner shops where we'd scrounge together loose change for snacks and then...

The spot.

I slow before I can stop myself.

Ben does too. His gaze flickers toward the alley beside the old bookshop—one that's been shut down for years, the windows plastered with To Let signs.

I don't need to look. I know what's there. The door to the back courtyard.

I know because it's where he first kissed me.

Not a chaste, sweet peck. Not an uncertain, shy brush of lips.

No. Ben Ashcroft kissed like he wanted to ruin me.

Oh he did.

We were seventeen. It was summer, and I'd just made some sarcastic remark, something about him being insufferable, and he'd just looked at me—looked at me—and then his hands were on my waist, my back pressed against the old wooden door, his mouth on mine, hot and hungry and reckless.

I remember gasping against his lips, the way his fingers dug into my hips, like he couldn't get close enough. The way I fisted his shirt, holding him there because I didn't want him to stop. Now the door is weathered and worn, chipped blue paint curling at the edges. It looks smaller. Less significant.

Funny how places change.

Funny how they don't.

"You remember," Ben murmurs, his voice low.

I keep my gaze straight ahead. "No idea what you're talking about."

His lips twitch, but he doesn't push.

Instead, he keeps walking, and I follow.

The sun is higher now, streaking gold through the treetops as we reach the far side of the park.

I hesitate again.

The fountain should be here. The old wishing well, cracked and moss-covered, where we used to throw in pennies and make ridiculous bets.

But it's gone.

Replaced by an empty stretch of concrete.

Ben frowns, scanning the space. "What happened?"

I exhale. "Funding cuts."

His brow furrows. "Seriously?"

I nod. "The council shut it down a few years ago. They said the maintenance costs weren't worth it."

Ben stares at the empty space for a long beat.

I don't know what I expect—some offhanded remark, some arrogant, 'not my problem' attitude.

Instead, he surprises me.

"That's bullshit," he mutters.

I blink. "Excuse me?"

His jaw tightens. "It was part of this park for decades. They can't just rip it out."

I fold my arms. "They can, and they did."

Ben's still staring, like he's cataloguing the loss, trying to piece together something that isn't there anymore.

For the first time in fifteen years, I see it—the boy I used to know.

The one who threw in coins just to make me laugh. The one who bet me a milkshake that I couldn't hit the centre with my eyes closed.

The one who promised me always.

I clear my throat, shoving the memory aside. "Not everything lasts forever, Ashcroft."

His gaze flicks to mine, something unreadable in his expression.

"Yeah," he says quietly. "I know."

For some stupid, stupid reason, that hurts.

We keep walking. I let the quiet stretch between us, let the streets we used to haunt guide us without thinking. It's only when I glance up—when I see the faded awning, the potted plants lined up by the window, the Bloom & Bean sign hanging slightly crooked—that I realise where we are.

I stop short.

Ben slows a second later. "Huh." His gaze flickers over the front of my cafe, taking in the details like he's seeing it for the first time.

Like he's actually seeing it.

"I didn't mean to..." I trail off, folding my arms, exhaling sharply. "We weren't supposed to end up here."

Ben doesn't look at me. He's still taking it in. The way the morning light catches on the glass. The way my mother's orchids are thriving in the window. The way the cafe, our cafe, has survived despite everything.

"This place..." he murmurs, voice barely above a whisper.

I don't move. I don't breathe.

He exhales, fingers trailing down the edge of the glass before curling into his palm. "It still smells the same."

My throat tightens.

I know what he means. Not just the scent of coffee and fresh flowers. But something deeper. The same feeling that wrapped around me every time I stepped inside as a child. The comfort, the warmth, the history.

The pieces of a life we once thought we'd share.

I should say something. Crack a joke. Deflect.

But the words stick, and for a split second, I let him have this.

Let myself have it, too.

Then he shifts, straightening, his hand falling away from the door. When he finally looks at me, there's something in his eyes—something raw.

Ben exhales slowly, his fingers flexing at his sides. Before I can name it, before I can let myself get pulled into it—

He steps back.

Not far. Just enough. Just enough to break whatever this is before it can become something else.

His jaw tightens, his gaze flicking over me once, unreadable, before he looks away.

"See you tonight," he says, voice smooth but distant. Then he turns on his heel and walks off, leaving me standing there, breathless, with nothing but the sound of his retreating footsteps.

The strangest, most infuriating feeling twists in my chest.

Because for the second time in fifteen years, Ben Ashcroft has walked away.

# 15

## Lila

I hate how much effort I've put into this.

The kitchen is spotless; the ingredients laid out in neat little bowls, everything prepped like I'm hosting some cooking show instead of enduring the longest, most infuriating two hours of my life.

The worst part? I actually spent time picking what we were going to bake.

At first, I was going to keep it simple—something foolproof, like scones. Quick, easy, impossible to mess up. Something that wouldn't require too much focus, because God knows I don't want to spend the evening actually enjoying this.

But as I stood there, flipping through the recipes, something inside me resisted.

Because baking has never been just a task for me. It's creation. Precision. The quiet magic of turning the simplest ingredients into something extraordinary. Even when I want to treat this night like a transaction—get in, get out, endure—I can't bring myself to choose something dull.

No. If I'm going to do this, I'm going to do it right.

Choux pastry.

It's demanding. A test of patience and skill. The kind of thing that needs care—that demands attention and maybe, just maybe, it'll keep us too busy to think about anything else.

I can already see it—Ben, sleeves rolled up, completely out of his depth, brow furrowed in concentration as he actually tries.

For some infuriating reason, that makes my chest go tight. At least this way, I get to distract myself. At least this way, I get to work. I should feel better. But then I catch my reflection in the cafe's window, and the self-satisfaction disappears immediately.

The dress was a mistake.

It's too much. Too fitted. Too... deliberate.

I should've just worn jeans and a sweater, something casual, something that didn't make it look like I actually thought about this.

Like I cared.

God, what was I thinking?

I shake my head, already turning on my heel. I can change. If I hurry, I can swap the dress for leggings and a hoodie, something that screams 'I did not put any effort into this, thank you very much.'

I start toward the stairs but then a sharp knock echoes through the cafe.

I freeze.

No.

No, no, no—he's early.

For half a second, I consider ignoring it. If I'm quiet enough, maybe he'll think I'm not ready and give me a few extra minutes to fix this mistake.

Then another knock. Slower this time. More deliberate.

"Come on, Lila. I know you're in there."

Shit.

I squeeze my eyes shut, inhaling deeply before turning back to the door.

I am not going to let him see that this threw me.

I am not going to let him see that I almost ran upstairs like a flustered idiot over a damn dress.

I am not—

I unlock the door and pull it open.

There he is.

Ben Ashcroft, standing in the glow of the street light, hands tucked into his coat pockets, his dark blond hair still slightly damp from his earlier shower. His stubble is sharper than usual, jawline crisp beneath the soft glow. His eyes flick over me, slow and assessing, and something about the way he lingers at my hemline makes my skin heat immediately.

His lips curve. "Nice dress."

I am going to kill him.

\*\*\*\*\*\*\*\*

Ben grips the piping bag, forearms flexing as he applies steady, controlled pressure. The dough flows out in perfect, even lines, smooth and precise.

I've got a front-row seat to a real-life thirst trap—like one of those unholy TikToks where a man smacks dough like it's foreplay, grips it like he's got sinful intentions, sniffs it for no damn reason except to make your knees weak, all while looking like six feet of heat, hunger, and pure filth.

Yet, here we are.

Ben completely focused on piping choux pastry is some kind

of sensory experience.

I force my gaze away. Anywhere but there.

"You're not going to critique my form?" he muses, not looking up.

His form?

This has to be some kind of cosmic test.

I clear my throat, praying to every deity available to not let my voice crack. "It's... adequate."

Ben's lips twitch, and he lifts a brow, still freakishly composed. "Adequate?"

I nod, refusing to let my eyes drop below his face. I will not get caught up in the way his fingers flex around that bag.

I will not.

He bites back a smile. "I can go harder."

I choke.

He squeezes the bag just a little too hard. The dough bursts out of the top, smearing across his wrist and forearm. I might pass out.

Ben exhales, annoyed but still too damn calm, wiping a streak of dough off his knuckles with his thumb. He licks his lips, studying the mess like it personally betrayed him.

"Guess I got a little carried away," he murmurs, turning his palm up, flexing his fingers against the sticky mess.

I make a strangled noise.

Abort. Abort.

This is not a normal reaction to someone ruining pastry.

Yet my brain? Absolute filth.

He looks up. Catches me staring.

His mouth curves. Knowing.

Shit.

I turn away so fast I nearly knock over the sugar bowl.

"That's—" My voice comes out too high. I clear my throat. "That's why I said even pressure."

Ben watches me, licking a bit of dough off his thumb.

I grab a towel and launch it at his face. "Clean yourself up."

He catches it one-handed, effortlessly, and I hate that it's impressive.

"Relax, sweetheart," he says, wiping off his hands. "It's just pastry."

No, it's not.

It's a trap. A freaking honey trap and I am not falling for it.

"Go wash up," I say, tossing him another towel, pretending I don't see the way his lips twitch. Pretending I'm not one more second away from completely losing my mind.

Ben catches it easily, but he doesn't move. Oh no. He leans against the counter like he's got all the time in the world, still watching me with that too-knowing, too-smug expression.

I narrow my eyes. "Sink. Now."

His brows lift, amusement flickering behind those dark eyes. "Bossy."

My pulse kicks up. Nope. We are not playing this game.

I tilt my head, raising a brow of my own. "I'd hate for the mighty Ben Ashcroft to be taken down by an unfortunate case of food poisoning."

His chuckle is low, warm. Dangerous. "Would you?"

I roll my eyes, refusing to answer that.

He finally moves, but not without dragging things out—stretching, rolling his shoulders, making his way to the sink with an irritating, slow swagger.

I regret everything.

The second he turns on the tap, I exhale sharply, rubbing my temples. The choux is in the oven. I just need to focus.

I glance at the counter. Right. Whipped cream. We need to prep the filling and then, like some divine, horrifying revelation, it hits me.

We have to pipe the cream into the choux buns.

I physically stop.

I blink at the mixing bowl, the piping bag sitting next to it like a loaded weapon.

How did I not realise this was the worst possible thing to make?

Ben's voice pulls me out of my spiral. "You okay over there?"

I snap my head up. Crap.

"Fine," I say too quickly. I grab the cream, shoving it in front of me like some kind of shield. It's fine. Everything is fine.

Ben dries his hands, walking back over, glancing at what's left to do. His smirk returns the second he sees the piping bag.

I feel the exact moment he pieces it together.

He picks up the piping bag, turning it over in his hands. His thumb pressing against the bag just enough to test the pressure.

"So," he drawls, flicking his gaze to me. "You want me to fill them up with cream?"

I short-circuit.

Because he says it with zero shame, zero hesitation, like this isn't the single worst baking decision I have ever made in my life.

I lock my jaw, I am not giving him the satisfaction. I am not reacting.

Instead, I glare daggers at him. "Yes, Ben. You take the nozzle, put it inside, and squeeze."

His lips twitch—barely—but I catch it.

Ben tilts his head, rolling up his sleeves a little higher, exposing strong forearms, the flex of tendons, veins trailing along tanned skin. He grips the piping bag like he's done this a thousand times before, adjusting his stance, focusing in a way that makes my stomach tighten.

He does it—slow, steady pressure, filling the pastry shell in one smooth, practiced movement.

I should not be watching this.

I should not be noticing the way his fingers curl around the bag, the effortless control, the slight furrow of concentration in his brow.

I should not be feeling my entire body burn from the inside out.

But I am.

I am dying.

Ben lifts a brow without looking at me. "You're very quiet, Lila."

I snap back to myself so fast I almost knock the bowl of cream onto the floor. "Just focused."

He hums, his smirk growing. "Uh-huh."

I spin toward the sink, flipping on the cold water so hard it splashes up the front of my dress. Fantastic. I press my wrists under the stream, trying to cool down, trying to regain some kind of control over my own brain.

Behind me, Ben chuckles under his breath.

"Told you this would be fun."

The bastard is enjoying this.

"You're surprisingly good at that," I mutter, focusing very hard on my own pastry, trying not to acknowledge the way his hands move, the way his shoulders flex, the way my brain is spiralling straight into the gutter.

Ben doesn't look up.

"Always been good with my hands."

Oh, for fuck's sake. Heat explodes under my skin.

I am not losing this round. Two can play that game.

Keeping my face completely unreadable, I dip my own finger into the cream. Slowly.

Then I drag my finger past my lips, tasting it.

Ben's jaw flexes.

I suck the cream off my finger slowly—deliberately—before pulling it free.

"Not bad," I murmur. "Could use more vanilla."

Ben doesn't move. Doesn't blink.

His grip on the piping bag tightens.

For the first time tonight, I have the upper hand. My victory is short lived.

BEEP. BEEP. BEEP!

The smoke alarm screeches through the kitchen.

"Shit!"

I whirl around, heart slamming, yanking open the oven door. Thick smoke billows out, curling toward the ceiling, the last batch of choux buns charred to hell.

Ben laughs, low and amused. Not helping.

"Maybe you should've set a timer, chef."

"Oh, shut up," I snap, reaching for the tray with a towel in my hand—and hiss as the heat bites into my hand as it catches the oven shelf.

Ben's smirk vanishes.

"Lila." His voice sharpens. "Did you just—"

"I'm fine," I mutter, shaking my hand out, ignoring the sting. "It's nothing—"

But Ben's already moving.

He grabs my wrist, firm but careful, turning my hand over. The skin is red, angry, the burn blooming fast.

His jaw locks.

Ben doesn't hesitate.

His grip tightens—not rough, but firm—as he guides me straight to the sink, flipping on the tap with his free hand.

Cool water rushes over my palm, sharp against the sting, but it's not what makes me suck in a breath.

It's him.

The way his fingers bracket my wrist, anchoring me there, his touch careful, possessive in a way that shouldn't make my stomach twist.

I don't know what's worse—the burn or the way his hands feel on me.

A different kind of heat spreads through my body, creeping up my spine, tightening in my chest.

I can't tell if I want to pull away or lean in.

That's dangerous.

Ben's jaw tics, his eyes locked on the angry flush of my skin.

"You should know better than to grab a tray like that," he murmurs, voice lower now, controlled but threaded with something else.

Concern? Frustration?

I scoff, trying to keep my voice even. "I'll add it to the list of life lessons."

Ben doesn't smile.

Instead, his thumb brushes just barely over the inside of my wrist, and my breath catches.

The water runs cold over my skin, but I feel scalded.

Finally, too soon and not soon enough, he reaches past me, shutting off the tap.

"Where's your first aid kit?"

I pull back. "Ben, it's not—"

"Where."

The weight in his voice stills me.

"Under the sink," I mutter, reluctantly.

Ben moves fast, retrieving it, pulling out burn cream and a cool compress, and before I can protest, he's taking my wrist again.

His touch is gentle. Careful. Infuriatingly tender.

I don't breathe as he smooths the cream over my skin, his fingers warm, steady, deliberate.

He doesn't say anything. Just studies my hand.

The new burn and the old ones, because I have plenty. Faded scars. Tiny imperfections. Cuts from knives, burns from trays, a history written on my skin. I force a laugh. "Occupational hazard. You should see my mum's hands. It's a family trait."

Ben doesn't laugh.

His fingers ghost over a particularly old scar, his brows drawing together.

"Lila..."

"It's just part of the job," I deflect, shaking my head. "You get used to it."

His grip tightens, just slightly. Just enough that I feel it.

Just enough that I freeze.

His eyes flick back to my hand. His fingers linger, skimming over an old scar, his jaw flexing. A breath. After a long, loaded beat—

He exhales.

Like something is breaking inside him.

Like something clicks.

When he finally speaks, his voice is quieter. Rougher. Like he's just now realising the truth himself.

"...I never should have left."

The words are soft. Not even a whisper.

But they wreck me.

My breath catches. My throat closes.

All this time—pretending it didn't matter. Of hating him for walking away and now?

Now he says this.

I don't think.

I can't think.

Because the next second, I'm kissing him.

Or maybe he kisses me.

I don't know who moves first, only that it's instant. Deep. Desperate.

His hands slide up my arms, fingers pressing into my waist, pulling me flush against him.

I fist his shirt, tilt my head, let him take more.

Because I need more.

I need all of him.

Ben groans into my mouth, the sound low, wrecked, his hands sliding into my hair, gripping tight.

He kisses me like he's starving.

Like I'm the first thing he's tasted in fifteen years that's real and I let him.

Because I'm starving too.

Because maybe I never stopped.

His tongue teases the seam of my lips, and I open for him, letting him in, letting him ruin me.

His hands skim low, dragging over my hips like he owns them, pulling me flush against him—closer, deeper, until I'm breathless and burning.

I barely register the moment he spins me, backing me against the counter. Cool marble bites through my dress, but his hands, his mouth—God, they're fire.

He palms my thigh, rough and desperate, shoving the hem of my dress higher. His fingers dig in like he's claiming territory, like he's daring me to stop him.

I don't.

His mouth breaks from mine, hot against my neck, jaw tight with restraint.

"Tell me," he growls, voice low and dangerous. "You're not married."

I freeze for half a second—heart hammering, breath caught in my throat.

He knows. Of course he does. He wouldn't be here if he didn't.

But it's not a question.

It's a demand.

A need.

His grip tightens, lips grazing the hollow of my throat. "Say it."

My pulse skitters. "I-I'm not."

His eyes burn into mine, wild and unrelenting. "Say it again."

I-I'm not married," I breathe, the words barely making it past my lips.

But it's not enough. Not for him.

His jaw clenches, a muscle ticking in his cheek as his gaze searches mine—dark, hungry, haunted.

"Is there anyone else?" His voice is low, guttural. "Anyone touching you? Anyone tasting you?"

I shake my head, breathless. "N-no. There's... there's no one."

His expression shatters—something raw and wrecked flickering through his eyes—and still, it's not enough.

"Tell me again."

My throat tightens. "There's no one else. J-just you."

A sound escapes him—half groan, half growl—and he's on me again, mouth crashing to mine like he's been holding back for years.

"Then I'm not stopping," he mutters against my lips. "Not this time."

I don't want him to.

Because we both know I never did.

Just like that, we're past the point of no return.

# 16

# Ben

I'm in a cafe filled with coffee, cream, sugar—all the things I should be craving.

Yet, the only thing I want to taste is her.

Lila.

She's pressed against the counter, lips swollen from my kisses, breath shallow, half-wrecked already.

I'm barely keeping it together.

My grip tightens on her thighs, spreading her open beneath me, my cock aching, throbbing, but it doesn't matter.

Not yet.

Because I'm not done.

Because I haven't tasted her.

The last time we were together it was our first time.

Our only time and as much as I've replayed it in my head—that night, that desperate, fumbling mess of firsts—it wasn't enough.

I was young, too impatient. I barely knew what the fuck I was doing.

Now, I know.

## BEN

Now I know exactly how to ruin her.

Lila shudders as my mouth trails down her neck, slow, deliberate, my fingers digging into the soft flesh of her thighs.

I nudge her knees wider.

She gasps, her head falling back against the cabinets, her fingers threading into my hair, gripping tight. She has no idea what's coming.

I lower myself onto my knees.

A fucking sacrilege considering the woman in front of me has made a sport out of pissing me off. But this is exactly where I want to be.

Lila is trembling, her breath ragged, the anticipation tangling with the frustration she won't admit. I run my hands up her legs, squeezing, feeling how soft she is, how warm.

She watches me, her lips parted, pupils blown wide.

I drag my mouth up the inside of her thigh, pressing a slow, open-mouthed kiss against the sensitive skin there. She jolts.

Fuck, she's sensitive.

She was always like this—all fire, all attitude—but beneath it?

She melts.

I look up at her, holding her gaze as I slide her dress higher, my fingers brushing over her bare skin.

"Ben..." her voice is shaky, almost unsure.

I hum against her thigh. "Relax, sweetheart. I'm about to make sure you never forget this."

Then, I taste her.

Lila arches off the counter, a strangled sound ripping from her throat as my tongue flicks against her.

Jesus fucking Christ.

I groan, gripping her hips tighter, pinning her down as she writhes beneath me.

She's so wet. So fucking perfect.

I bury myself deeper, my tongue lapping, teasing, pushing her higher.

She's shaking, her thighs tensing, gripping, trying to keep control.

But she's losing.

I suck her clit into my mouth, flicking my tongue just right—

"Oh, God—"

Her breath hitches. I feel it.

She's close.

I slide two fingers inside her, stretching, curling, hitting exactly where she needs me.

She gasps—shatters—falls apart in my hands.

She comes hard and I fucking love it.

Love the way she trembles, the way her hands fist in my hair, the way she whimpers my name like she never stopped belonging to me.

I grin against her, dragging it out, letting her ride it, my tongue lapping up every fucking drop like I'm starved for her.

Because I am.

Because I always was.


She's still shaking when I stand, still panting when I kiss her—deep, letting her taste herself on my tongue.

She moans into my mouth, her nails scraping down my chest, desperate for more and fuck if that doesn't drive me insane.

I pull her hips forward, grinding against her, letting her feel exactly what she does to me.

I'm so fucking hard, it's painful.

I need more.

I need all of her.

My hands slide up her thighs, pushing fabric aside, preparing to undo my belt—

BANG. BANG. BANG.

"Lila? Are you in there?"

Lila freezes.

I go still.

Her entire body locks up.

No.

No fucking way.

"No, no, no—" Lila shoves at my shoulders, hard.

"Ben," she whispers, panicked. "You have to go."

The fuck I do.

I grip the counter, bracing myself, my body still humming from her, from what just happened.

"You've got to be kidding me."

Lila scrambles off the counter like she's just woken up from a bad dream.

Like she didn't just fall apart in my hands.

Like she isn't still fucking trembling from me.

She adjusts her dress, running a shaking hand through her hair as she rushes to the cafe's security monitor mounted near the back. I barely register what's happening—because my blood is still in my cock, my body still wired from her, my fingers still fucking coated in her.

But then, she goes pale.

"Shit," she hisses under her breath.

I push off the counter, rolling my shoulders back. "Who the

hell is it?"

She doesn't answer, just angles the screen toward me.

Mrs Herbert.

The name alone makes something twist in my chest.

The old woman stands outside, peering through the glass door, her purse clutched in front of her. My old neighbour from when I used to live here. Of all people.

Lila whirls toward me, eyes wild. "Stay in the back and don't come out!"

I stare at her. She's serious.

"You're joking."

Her expression hardens. "Ben, I swear to God—"

I grit my teeth, jaw flexing. I should tell her no. Should tell her I don't hide from anyone.

But then I see it.

The sheer panic in her face.

Not just about getting caught. Something else. Something deeper and that's how I find myself hiding in the back of the cafe like some teenager, barely keeping my shit together.

I hear the front bell chime as Lila unlocks it.

"Oh, Mrs Herbert," she says, voice still slightly breathless. "What are you doing here so late?"

The old woman sighs, stepping inside. "I couldn't sleep, dear. Kept thinking about this awful development proposal." Her voice wavers. "I wanted to make sure I signed the petition before it's too late."

Silence.

Then Lila murmurs, "That's very kind of you."

Mrs Herbert sighs. "Not kind, Lila. Necessary. This cafe—this whole row of businesses—it's been a lifeline for people like me. I lost my husband five years ago, and coming here, seeing you, seeing the others, having somewhere to go... It's kept me going."

My chest tightens.

The weight of her words sits heavy.

"It's not just me," Mrs Herbert continues, her voice lower now, raw. "Do you know how many people rely on this place? On all of you? I don't understand why someone would want to take that away."

I swallow hard.

Lila exhales, and I can hear the emotion in her voice. "Me neither."

Fuck.

I lean back against the shelves, pressing the heels of my hands into my eyes.

This wasn't supposed to happen.

This wasn't supposed to be personal.

I didn't get where I am by letting shit like this get to me.

Now, I'm hiding in a back room, my body still wrecked from touching Lila, listening to a woman pour her heart out about how my fucking project is about to gut the very place she's built her life around.

I clench my jaw, pressing my fingers into my temples as Mrs Herbert's words echo in my head.

*A lifeline.*

*Kept me going.*

I exhale sharply through my nose. No.

They're wrong.

They don't see the long-term benefits. The opportunities.

They don't see—

But then, a quiet voice in the back of my head mutters. *What if you don't see it either?*

I shut it down. I can make her understand. She just has to listen.

I can show her—show all of them—that this isn't about gutting their community. It's about elevating it. Creating something sustainable, something better. A future, not a stagnant memory.

She just needs to trust me.

She just needs to let me explain.

The door chimes again, and I hear Mrs Herbert murmur her goodbyes. Footsteps shuffle toward the back, and then—

Lila steps inside.

She freezes the second she sees me and in an instant, I know.

No.

She's shutting down.

I see it in the way her shoulders tense, the way she wraps her arms around herself like she's trying to hold something—everything—together.

The warmth in her eyes? Gone.

That soft, breathless haze from before? Gone.

All that's left is ice.

She inhales, exhales. Slow. Measured.

"This was a mistake."

The words hit like a punch to the ribs.

"Lila—"

"You have to go."

I step toward her, but she holds up a hand, fingers shaking just slightly. "Ben, just—please."

*Please.*

I've heard her say it before.

All those years ago.

This isn't a plea for me to stay—it's a demand for me to leave.

For me to let her go.

I clench my jaw so tight it aches. My hands curl into fists at my sides. Everything inside me is screaming to fix this, to pull her back, to remind her what just happened, what we just had—and just like that, the anger starts to burn.

Not the frustration I've been wrestling with all night.

No, this is different.

Because I let her in.

Because I kissed her like she was still mine. Tasted her. Worshipped her.

Now she's shutting down like it never happened. Like I never happened.

For the first time, it hits me. Maybe this was the plan all along, this was what she wanted—her revenge. Fifteen fucking years, and I walked straight into her trap like the lovesick idiot I swore I'd never be again.

A sharp laugh escapes me, bitter and breathless.

"Right." I exhale, shaking my head as I take a step back. "You got what you wanted, huh?"

Lila stiffens. "What? No! Ben—"

I don't let her finish.

I swipe my coat off the chair, shove my arms through the sleeves, barely feeling the movement. My blood is still pounding, my pulse still wrecked from her, from what we just did.

But fuck her.

Fuck this whole night.

I storm past her, heading straight for the door.

She doesn't stop me.

She doesn't even try.

The bell above the cafe door jingles as I yank it open, the night air rushing in, biting cold against my heated skin.

I don't look back.
Not this time.
Not ever again.

# 17

## Ben

I should be over this by now.

It's been days since Lila pushed me away. Days since she shut me out and shut me the fuck down.

I'm still pissed.

Because no matter how much I try to focus on the goddamn project, on the business, on anything else, I can't stop thinking about her.

The way she unravelled beneath me.

The way she begged for more.

The way she looked at me afterward—like I was a mistake she was desperate to erase.

I grit my teeth, gripping the pen in my hand so hard I half expect it to snap.

"You want to run that by me again?" James asks, one brow arched, tone laced with disbelief and a healthy dose of sarcasm.

I don't bother looking up from the contract. "Increase the offer."

Silence.

Then a low whistle. "Okay, who are you and what have you

done with Ben Ashcroft?"

I keep my eyes on the page. "You heard me."

James leans forward, tapping the table with his pen. "We're already offering over market. You planning to buy her a castle too, or just the whole goddamn street?"

I glance up, slowly. "Did I ask for your opinion, or just your signature?"

He grins, unfazed. "Relax, I'm just saying—bit out of character, that's all. I checked her company out, you know—Bloom & Brew. Solid setup. Good branding and yeah... she's hot as hell."

Something sharp flares in my chest.

James doesn't notice it at first—or maybe he does, the bastard—because he keeps going. "Didn't peg you as the type to let a pretty face scramble your business sense. Unless this is one of those situations where your cock's doing the talking—"

The chair scrapes hard as I shove back from the table.

His grin slips. "Whoa—alright, easy. I was kidding."

I stare him down, jaw tight. "Don't talk about her like that."

A beat of silence.

Then James blinks. "Jesus. You're serious."

I don't answer. I don't need to.

He sits back, still watching me carefully. "Alright... noted."

I rake a hand through my hair, jaw clenched, the burn in my chest refusing to go out. "It's a business move."

"Sure," James says lightly, but I can hear the shift in his voice—something more thoughtful, more cautious now. "Just making sure you're still the one steering the ship."

"I just want it done."

He nods slowly, tapping the pen against the table again. "Fine. I'll push it through."

"Good."

James leans back, arching a brow. "But if you start buying her flowers and quoting poetry, I'm staging an intervention."

I glare at him.

He grins again. "See? Now that's the Ben I know."

But even he knows it's not.

Not anymore.

This is the best move. Get the deal sorted. Get the hell out of here.

Just like before.

I grab my phone, checking my emails. Not a single one from her.

Not that I expected anything—Lila made herself clear. I haven't stepped foot in the cafe since. Not even walked past. Not even had a decent coffee. Maybe that's what's really pissing me off. Not the rejection. Not the guilt.

Just caffeine withdrawal.

Right.

I scrub a hand down my face, rolling my neck, trying to shake the tension sitting like lead in my chest. I need to stop thinking about this. Need to focus.

But before I go—before I leave this town for good—there's one thing left to do.

I glance at my watch, push back from the desk, and grab my coat.

Because it's been too many years.

It's time.

\*\*\*\*\*

The graveyard is quiet.

Too quiet.

The kind of quiet that seeps into your bones, filling the spaces between your ribs with something you don't want to name.

The early signs of spring are everywhere—snowdrops scattered across the grass, delicate and unbothered by the weight of the past. The sunlight filters through the yew trees, long golden streaks cutting across mossy headstones, casting soft, shifting shadows. The air is crisp, carrying that damp, earthy scent of old stone and fresh growth.

It doesn't belong here.

Spring. Renewal.

Not in a place built on endings.

I shove my hands into my coat pockets, my jaw locking as I take the last few steps toward the grave.

Too many years. Too many excuses.

It was never the right time. Never convenient. Never necessary.

But it was all bullshit, wasn't it?

The headstone is the same as it always was—plain, worn at the edges, the carved letters softened by time. My mother never wanted anything fancy. Never liked to make a fuss. Just the basics, Ben, she'd say. No need to be dramatic.

I exhale sharply through my nose.

If only she could see me now, standing here like a fucking idiot, years too late, with nothing to say.

I drag a hand through my hair, fingers tightening at the back of my neck.

"Hey, mum."

The words feel wrong. Stupid. Too small for the weight in my chest.

## BEN

I glance down, and that's when I see it.

Flowers.

Fresh ones.

Not the sad, store-bought kind, but real, careful arrangements. Small bundles of wildflowers and soft white snowdrops, wrapped in twine, placed neatly at the base of the headstone. Nestled among them—sweet peas.

I stare at them, my pulse slowing, the air around me shifting.

Someone's been here.

Someone's been coming here.

A lump forms in my throat, heavy and unexpected, my chest tightening as I kneel, brushing my fingers over the delicate petals.

"I was wondering when you'd show up."

I turn.

Mr Hamilton stands a few feet away, hands in his coat pockets, his weathered face unreadable. The last time I saw him, I was seventeen. A kid drowning in grief, visiting this place like it was the only thing keeping me tethered.

I straighten, nodding once. "Mr Hamilton."

He studies me for a long beat, then exhales. "Been a while."

I nod again, not trusting myself to speak.

He steps closer, his eyes flicking down to the flowers. "Figured you'd want to know."

I frown. "Know what?"

He tilts his head. "Who's been bringing them."

I already know.

My throat tightens. "Lila—"

Mr Hamilton doesn't blink. "Every holiday, like clockwork."

I inhale sharply through my nose, turning away, dragging a hand over my mouth. Lila.

All these years. She never stopped.

She never stopped caring, even when I did.

I swallow hard, my heart pounding in my chest, the weight of everything suddenly crushing.

Mr Hamilton watches me carefully. "She never said much. Just left the flowers, stood there for a few minutes, and went on her way."

I clench my jaw, trying to breathe past the tightness in my chest.

His voice lowers. "But the way she looked at that headstone?" He shakes his head. "She never stopped missing you, son."

My stomach turns, something raw scraping against my ribs.

I should have fucking known.

I look back at the flowers.

Sweet peas. Mum's favourites. My mother was allergic to most flowers—pollen gave her headaches, made her eyes water. But sweet peas? They were safe. No heavy scent, no sneezing fits. She always said they were the only flowers she'd ever let me bring inside as a kid.

I swallow hard.

Lila would remember that.

Of course she would.

She paid attention to things most people overlooked. The little details. The things that mattered.

Even the things I'd let myself forget.

A goddamn punch to the gut and in that moment—I know.

I can't leave.

Not like this.

Not again.

Because I finally get it.

She didn't push me away because she hated me. She pushed me away because she was scared. Scared I'd leave again. Scared I'd destroy her all over again. She kept coming here, she remembered. My hands fist at my sides, my heart pounding harder, my pulse roaring in my ears.

I need to fix this.

I need to fix everything.

Hamilton exhales, stepping back. "Whatever happened between you two..." He nods toward the flowers. "You still have time."

I clench my jaw, my fists tight at my sides. For a moment, I look at Mr Hamilton—not as the caretaker from my childhood, but as a kid again, hoping someone will tell me it's not too late. That I haven't missed my chance.

His gaze holds mine, steady and knowing. Like he already believes I can fix this—even if I'm not sure myself.

But I don't wait.

I turn and walk away, purpose surging through me.

Because Lila Ng is mine.

This time, I'm not fucking leaving without her.

# 18

## Ben

*Soft, bare skin pressed against mine. The slow, steady rise and fall of her breath.*

*Lila.*

*My head is heavy on the pillow, my entire body languid, sated in a way I've never felt before. I exhale slowly, eyes still closed, my fingers tracing lazy circles against her back. She shifts, murmuring something incoherent, nuzzling into my chest.*

*I smirk, cracking an eye open. "Tired, sweetheart?"*

*She makes a sound that's half a sigh, half a laugh. "Shut up."*

*I chuckle, tightening my arm around her, feeling the weight of her against me. Jesus. This is real.*

*We did it.*

*After months of waiting, of holding back, of being careful—tonight, she was mine. And it was everything.*

*She's still tucked against me, her fingers idly tracing over my ribs, completely at peace and for the first time, so am I.*

*Until it happens.*

*BANG. BANG. BANG.*

*I jolt upright.*

## BEN

*The knocking is loud. Insistent.*

*My heart slams against my ribs as I glance at the clock—3:27 a.m.*

*What the hell?*

*Lila stirs, eyes fluttering open. "What was that?"*

*BANG. BANG. BANG.*

*A voice cuts through the night.*

*"Ben! Open the damn door!"*

*I freeze.*

*No.*

*Not him. Not now.*

*My jaw clenches, rage crackling through me like a live wire. Drunk, no doubt. Here to give me shit about Lila. Like he has any right.*

*I shove out of bed, yanking on my jeans so fast I nearly trip. Lila stirs beside me, already reaching for her robe, her wide eyes flickering with worry.*

*I catch her wrist before she can move. "Stay here." My voice is low, firm. "It's my dad. He's drunk, and I don't want you anywhere near this."*

*Her brows knit together. "Ben—"*

*"Please, Lila." I don't wait for an argument. I don't need her seeing him like this—slurring, swaying, reeking of booze and bad decisions. I don't need her witnessing the man who calls himself my father, especially not in this state.*

*She hesitates, but I don't. I let go of her and turn away, storming out of the room, my pulse hammering.*

*The pounding continues, shaking the damn door.*

*Bang. Bang. Bang.*

*Fucking relentless.*

*I take the stairs two at a time. If he thinks he can show up here and start spewing his usual bullshit, he's about to find out exactly how done I am with him.*

*I rip the door open, my glare burning hot. "What the fuck do you want?"*

*The words are barely out of my mouth before I register the look on his face.*

*Not just drunk.*

*Something else.*

*His eyes are bloodshot. Not just from booze, but from something raw, something hollow. His chest heaves like he ran here, his hands shaking at his sides.*

*"You didn't answer your goddamn phone." His voice is rough, thick with something unfamiliar—grief. "Me, the hospital—we called a hundred fucking times."*

*A sick feeling slams into my gut.*

*No.*

*My dad sways, runs a trembling hand over his face. "It's your mother, Ben." His voice cracks. "She's gone."*

*The words don't make sense. They hit, but they don't sink in. They just hover there, weightless, waiting for my brain to catch up.*

*I shake my head. "What are you talking about?"*

*"Car accident." His throat bobs, and for the first time in my life, my father looks small. Broken. "She—she didn't make it."*

*The world tilts.*

*No.*

*No, no, no.*

*Cold washes over me, creeping in like ice beneath my skin.*

*"You're lying." The words are barely a whisper. A plea.*

*His face twists with something sharp. "You think I'd fucking lie about this?"*

*I stagger back, my mind scrambling, searching for something—anything—to make this untrue. To undo it.*

*Then it hits me.*
*My phone.*
*I turned it off.*
*I shut it down so I could be with Lila, so I wouldn't have to deal with anything outside of her.*
*I wasn't there.*
*I wasn't fucking there.*
*A sharp, strangled breath rips through my chest. My hands curl into fists, nails biting into my palms, but I don't feel it. I don't feel anything.*
*She's gone.*
*I missed her last moments.*

\*\*\*\*\*\*\*\*

The Closed sign stares back at me from the cafe door.

Locked.

Not a problem.

I rap my knuckles against the glass. Once. Twice.

Inside, Lila stiffens.

She's behind the counter, shoulders tense, wiping down trays like they personally offended her. Like she didn't just hear me.

She did.

I knock again, slower this time. More deliberate.

Her head snaps up, and the second her eyes meet mine, something flickers.

Annoyance. Frustration. Maybe something else.

Good. I'd rather have her pissed than indifferent.

She exhales sharply, shaking her head like she's already regretting whatever choice she's about to make. Then she moves to the door, flipping the lock with quick, sharp motions before yanking it open just enough to glare at me.

"What part of closed do you not understand?"

I step forward, careful—gentler—but close enough that she has to meet my eyes.

"The part where you think I'd just walk away."

Her fingers tighten around the door, like she's bracing herself. Like she's one second from shutting me out completely.

"I don't have time for this." Her voice is clipped, impatient. But beneath it? There's something else. Something frayed.

I keep my voice steady. "Then make time."

She exhales sharply, frustration flickering across her face. "Ben—"

"I just need you to listen." My throat tightens, but I don't move back. "I won't stay if you don't want me to. But I'm not leaving without saying what I came here to say."

Her jaw clenches. She looks past me, toward the empty street, weighing her options. Calculating.

She doesn't want this. Doesn't want me here.

But she also doesn't tell me to go, and that's enough.

With a sharp breath, she steps back, pushing the door open just enough to let me through. "Five minutes."

I step inside.

The lock clicks.

Not a win.

Just a chance.

Don't fuck this up.

The silence stretches between us, thick and suffocating.

Lila crosses her arms, her posture screaming impatience, but her fingers flex against her sleeve—just once. A flicker of something beneath the anger.

I open my mouth. Nothing comes out.

## BEN

Fuck.

I rake a hand through my hair, exhaling sharply. "I—I shouldn't have left like that."

She lifts a brow. "Which time?"

My jaw tightens.

I take a breath, steadying myself. "I was pissed, Lila. I thought—" I shake my head, trying to piece the words together. "I thought you were just trying to get back at me."

Her eyes go wide, fury crackling like a live wire. "Are you fucking kidding me?"

Before I can react, she shoves me. Hard.

"The fucking irony, Ben." Another shove. Sharper. "You thought I was trying to get back at you?"

My ribs ache, but not from the impact—from her anger, her pain, all of it crashing into me.

I don't move. I let her.

Her breath is ragged, her fingers curling into fists. "You're the one trying to rip everything away from me." She shoves me again. "You're the one throwing money at our business, our home, trying to make us disappear like we're just some fucking inconvenience—and you have the audacity to stand here and say you thought I was out for revenge?"

She laughs, bitter and hollow. It's the worst fucking sound I've ever heard.

She shakes her head, a humourless smile twisting her lips. "Oh, come on, spare me the act."

What?

My stomach twists, my breath stalling in my chest. "Lila, what the fuck are you talking about?" My pulse pounds, confusion slamming into me like a freight train. "Lila, I—"

She doesn't let me finish.

Her jaw clenches, her breath coming fast and uneven. "That night—" Her voice falters, and she exhales sharply, pressing the heels of her hands into her eyes before looking at me again, gaze burning. "Fifteen years ago—it was a mistake."

A cold, sharp pain rips through my chest. Like a blade, buried deep.

I don't move. I can't.

Her voice shakes, but she doesn't stop. "I should have never—" She swallows, forcing herself to keep going, even as I watch her break. "You would have been with your mum."

My blood turns ice cold. No.

Her voice catches, and she looks away, jaw clenched like she's trying to keep herself from breaking. "And now you're back. Tearing down the last thing I have left. Isn't that what you wanted, Ben?"

Her eyes snap back to mine, and I see it.

Not just the anger.

Not just the fight.

The guilt.

The weight of fifteen fucking years pressing down on her, twisting everything, making her believe—actually believe—that I've been trying to destroy her because of something she had no control over.

She's been holding onto this guilt this whole time and it wrecks me.

The grief, the guilt, the weight of the us that was ripped apart that night—she never let it go.

Just like I never fucking did.

"Lila," my voice is hoarse, raw, but she shakes her head.

"No." She blinks, a tear slipping free, but she doesn't let it fall. She won't let herself. "You don't get to stand here and tell me I'm wrong. You don't get to tell me you don't hate me."

My chest caves.

"I don't." I step forward, voice thick. "I never did. I never could."

She laughs, wrecked and breathless, shaking her head, refusing to believe it. "Then why are you doing this?" Her voice cracks. "Why are you taking this place from me?"

I can't breathe.

She's staring at me—demanding answers I don't fucking have.

I open my mouth. Nothing comes out.

Because I don't know how to explain it. I don't know where to fucking start.

My chest tightens, pulse pounding in my ears, heat rising fast and sharp up my throat.

Why?

Because I wasn't there.

Because I missed my mother's last breath while Lila—Lila—was looking at me like I was her whole goddamn world.

Because I turned off my phone. Because I thought I had time. Because I was seventeen and arrogant and didn't know what loss looked like until I walked through that door and found out I was too fucking late.

She was gone.

My father—useless, drunk, hollow—looked at me like it was *my* fault. Like I was supposed to fix everything.

When I couldn't? He stopped trying. Not all at once, but in pieces—quiet, steady decay. He let the house rot. Let the bills pile up. Let the debt swallow us whole.

I tried. I *tried*, Lila.

I worked. Any job I could find. I held it all together until it all slipped through my fingers anyway.

The house—gone.

The life I thought we had—gone.

I was just a kid, standing in the ruins, with nothing left to give.

No home. No future. No plan.

Lila?

She was everything I couldn't keep.

Everything I didn't deserve.

So I left.

Not because I didn't love her—but because I did. Because I couldn't stand to look at her and know what I'd lost. Because pride—stupid, reckless pride—convinced me it was better to walk away than let her see how far I'd fallen.

Now she's standing here, looking at me like I'm some villain hell-bent on destroying her world, when all I've ever done is destroy mine.

Something hot and violent burns in my chest.

I reach blindly for the nearest object—a cup—hurling it across the room. It shatters against the wall, shards scattering across the floor.

Lila jumps.

"You think I'd burn everything down just to get even? You think I hate you that much?"

Her breath stutters, but she says nothing.

So I keep going. Voice low, wrecked. Raw.

"I don't hate you, Lila. I never fucking did."

She looks at me, stricken. Lost.

She swallows, but she doesn't answer.

That's all it takes for me to break.

## BEN

I let out a sharp breath, hands flexing at my sides. Lila's brows pull together, and I shake my head, laughing bitterly, running a hand over my face like I can scrub away the weight pressing down on me.

She wants the truth?

She can have it.

I step even closer, towering over her, forcing her to see the wreckage she left behind.

Her breath catches.

"You want to know the real reason I left?" My voice drops lower, rougher. "Because I couldn't stand being near you."

She flinches, and it guts me. But I'm too far gone to stop now.

"I couldn't look at you without thinking about everything I lost. Everything I should have had. You were the one thing in my life that felt real, and I—" My throat closes, but I force the words out. "I couldn't have you."

She blinks, her breath shuddering. "Ben..."

I laugh, but it's hollow. Dark. Fucking broken.

"You were everything good, and I was drowning." I shake my head. "You deserved better."

She stares at me, eyes wide, raw, full of something I can't name.

Her face twists, her hands trembling, her lips parting like she's about to say something.

But she doesn't.

She just breaks and fuck, I feel it.

Like a live wire sparking between us, like something that's been stretched too tight for too long finally snaps.

I don't think.

I move.

I grab her. Pull her in. Drag her into me, against me, into this fucking mess of who we are.

Her breath stutters, but I don't stop.

I press my forehead to hers, my pulse roaring, my hands shaking as I grip her waist, holding on like she's the only thing keeping me from coming undone.

My voice is raw, hoarse, wrecked.

"I've never stopped thinking about you."

Lila lets out a sharp exhale, like the words hit her straight in the chest. Like they destroy her.

Her hands tighten on my shirt, her whole body tensed, conflicted, fucking unravelling.

"All these years, Lila." I shake my head, my breath ragged, lips barely brushing hers. "I tried to forget. I tried to move on. I tried—" My throat locks up, but I force it out. "But I never stopped."

A choked sound escapes her. A gasp. A sob. A plea. Her fingers fist my shirt, yanking me closer, and I groan into her mouth, my hands sliding into her hair, tilting her head back so I can devour her.

I feel her shudder. Feel her surrender.

Because this isn't careful.

This is pent-up rage and years of regret.

This is everything we've never said, everything we've never let ourselves feel.

I back her up against the counter, her legs parting as I step between them, pressing against her, grounding myself in her.

She moans, soft and breathless, and fuck, it wrecks me.

I drag my lips from hers, pressing kisses down her jaw, her throat, the place where her pulse is hammering, just as frantic as mine.

Her hands slide into my hair, pulling, needing, holding. I

know it now.

I feel it now.

Lila's breath is ragged, her body pressed tight against mine, but neither of us pulls away.

There's no hesitation.

No second-guessing.

Just need.

Raw. Overwhelming. Undeniable.

I grab her thighs, lifting her onto the counter, her legs wrapping around me like she's meant to be there.

Her nails dig into my shoulders, her chest rising and falling in sharp, uneven breaths. Her lips are swollen, her eyes—dark, hungry—but more than that, wrecked.

Just like me.

I can't stop.

I don't even try.

My hands are on her, pushing up her skirt, shoving fabric out of the way, needing—

Fuck. I can't breathe.

This isn't about patience.

This isn't about teasing.

This is years of longing, years of loss, years of fucking restraint snapping all at once.

I fumble with my jeans, yanking them open, every muscle in my body tightly coiled, aching.

Lila gasps as I grip her hips, my forehead pressed against hers, our breaths tangled, our bodies trembling.

She shifts, aligns and then—I'm inside her.

Deep.

Home.

Lila cries out, her head falling back, her fingers clutching me like she'll never let go.

I let out a strangled groan, my arms bracing against the counter, holding us both together, because fuck she's tight, she's warm, she's everything and I'm already losing my mind.

Her legs tighten around me, her hips tilting, desperate for more and I give it to her.

Fast. Hard. Right.

She clings to me, gasping my name, shaking with every thrust.

The cafe is silent except for the sound of us—harsh breaths, desperate moans, bodies colliding, breaking, burning.

It's reckless. It's rushed.

But it's also inevitable.

Her fingers curl at the back of my neck, dragging me down, kissing me like she needs me to survive. Maybe we both do.

I press my forehead against hers, my breath ragged, my hands tightening around her waist, holding her exactly where I need her.

"You feel this?" I growl, voice raw, desperate. "This is real. This is us."

She whimpers, her legs locked around me, pulling me deeper, demanding more.

I give it to her.

"You were made for me." My voice is a snarl, my lips brushing hers, teasing, taunting, owning.

Her head falls back, a wrecked moan tearing from her throat.

I drag my teeth over her jaw, biting down just enough to make her cry out, to make her feel me.

"Mine—"

Her entire body trembles, tightens, fucking bows into me.

"Say it," I growl, breath hot, breathless. "Say it, Lila."

Her voice is wrecked, shattered, trembling on a whimper.

"I was always yours."

I lose it.

I slam into her harder, rougher, hungrier—like it's not just her body I want, but her soul. Like I'm trying to bury myself inside her, claim her from the inside out, until there's no space left that doesn't have my name carved into it.

The sound of us is savage—wet, filthy, desperate. Skin slapping. Breaths breaking. Curses whispered between clenched teeth.

I slide a hand into her hair, tilting her head back, forcing her to see me, to feel me, to know this isn't just sex.

It's a fucking undoing.

A surrender.

I watch her fall apart, feel her tighten around me, her body clenching, trembling, wrecked. It slams into me, a violent, blinding, full-body release that knocks the breath from my lungs, rips a guttural, raw, fucking primal sound from my throat.

I bury myself deep, my entire body locking up, shaking, burning as I spill into her, wave after wave of pure, uncontrollable pleasure tearing through me.

It's not just an orgasm.

It's an exorcism.

Like fifteen years of want, of need, of frustration finally breaking free, ripping me apart, leaving me ruined inside her.

I sag against her, my forehead pressing into her shoulder, my chest heaving, my hands still gripping her like I can't let go.

Because I can't.

Because I never fucking could.

# 19

# Ben

Some things don't need fire to burn. They just need a little oxygen. I stand across the road from his office, arms folded, watching the man through the glass. Derrick Crayton, slumped in his fake leather chair like he still owns the world, barking down the phone like he's untouchable. Like he didn't throw a grieving boy and his alcoholic father out of their home fifteen years ago. No warning. No grace period. Just a notice letter and a shrug.

"Business is business," he said.

I've never forgotten. Back then, I had no voice. No power. Just a mother buried too soon and a father slowly drowning in grief and whisky.

Now?

Now I have power in spades.

I didn't need to make a scene. Didn't need to put my name on anything. Just a few discreet phone calls. A few well-placed whispers. A tip-off to the right authorities. Fire safety violations. Substandard electrical work. Illegal evictions. Unregistered tenancy deposits. Undeclared income. Tax irregularities. Turns out, when you've spent years cutting corners and screwing over your tenants, all it takes is one person to pull the right thread — and the whole fucking operation starts to unravel.

The tenants aren't going anywhere. They're protected now. Most of them don't even know why the council and the housing standards team have suddenly taken such a keen interest in their building. Why inspectors keep turning up with clipboards and stern expressions. Why enforcement letters keep landing on Crayton's desk faster than he can rip them open.

I'm not dismantling his business. I'm just exposing it.

The truth?

The truth will do far more damage than I ever could with a cheque.

Fines. Investigations. Frozen assets. Lawsuits.

Soon enough, his name will be poison in this town.

I could've bought him out. Could've walked in there, signed a cheque, and watched him squirm. But that would've been too easy. No, this way is better.

Because he won't even know it was me.

Not until the headlines hit.

Not until his lawyer stops returning his calls and his bank account is locked down.

Not until he realises his empire is built on sand—and someone just pulled the tide in.

Even then... he'll never be able to prove a damn thing.

I turn and walk away, slipping my hands into my coat pockets. The late afternoon air is crisp, clean, and sharp.

I don't need credit. I don't need thanks.

I just needed justice.

Finally, he's getting what he deserves.

Quiet. Legal. Ruthless.
Exactly how I like it.

# 20

# Lila

My body is deliciously sore, every inch of me humming with the memories of last night. After the kitchen, twice in my apartment. A deep, satisfied ache settles into my limbs, but the warmth spreading through my chest is what really does me in.

It wasn't just sex.

It was something else entirely. Something I refuse to name. Something dangerous.

I stretch, rolling onto my side, reaching for him—

But the space beside me is empty.

My stomach drops.

I push up on my elbows, blinking away sleep, scanning the dim light filtering through my apartment. No sound of the shower running. No rustle of movement. Just me.

Alone.

He left.

A lump lodges in my throat as panic kicks up, irrational and sharp. I don't know what I expected, but waking up alone wasn't it.

I press my fingers against my temples, forcing down the sting in my chest. Had last night meant more to me than it did to him? Was I just a closure fuck? A goodbye?

Then, I see it.

A single note on the pillow beside me. Folded. Neat. Precise.

Meet me at the park at 12.

No explanation. No apology. Just a request. I suck in a shaky breath, my chest tightening.

What have I done?

*****

The park is buzzing when I arrive. I scan the crowd, my pulse kicking up as I spot Clara near the front, arms crossed, her face unreadable. Thomas is speaking with a few of the other business owners, but no one looks particularly pleased. I step closer, clearing my throat. "Clara? What's going on?"

She turns, lifting a brow. "Wish I knew. Ben just called everyone here. No one seems to have a clue what for."

My stomach twists.

I glance at the gathered crowd, the uneasy expressions, the way everyone murmurs to each other, waiting. The uncertainty coils around my ribs, squeezing tighter. If no one knows why we're here then this could be anything and I'm not sure I'm ready for what that means.

Then I see him—Ben, standing where the fountain once stood, his hands tucked into his pockets. He looks calm, composed, but I know better. There's tension in his shoulders, a weight in his stance.

He turns when he sees me, something shifting in his gaze, but he doesn't falter.

"I called you all here today because I owe you an apology,"

he begins, voice steady. "And a promise."

A murmur ripples through the small crowd, but no one interrupts.

Ben continues, meeting their eyes one by one. "I came here with a plan that I thought made sense. A business decision. But I didn't stop to think about the people it would affect." He exhales, shaking his head. "That was a mistake."

Someone scoffs. "A big mistake."

A few chuckles follow, but Ben doesn't flinch. Instead, Clara crosses her arms, lifting a sceptical brow. "So, what? You just woke up this morning and decided to grow a conscience?"

Ben lets out a breath, nodding. "Something like that."

Thomas scoffs. "Convenient timing."

Eva chimes in, arms folded. "You've put us through hell these last few months, Ben. You can't expect us to just roll over and be grateful."

Ben meets their stares head-on. "I don't. I know I messed up. I know I've been a complete bastard about all of this. But I want to fix it and I'm willing to prove that this isn't just some PR move." He pauses. "I get that words aren't enough. So, let me show you."

Clara exchanges a glance with Thomas, then sighs. "You better, because if you pull something like this again, I swear to God, I will personally make sure your hair never looks good in this town again."

Ben smirks slightly. "Terrifying. Truly." Instead, he nods. "Yeah. I deserve that."

He glances at me then, just for a second, before turning back to the group. "I'm cancelling the development. Instead, I'll be reallocating the investment to support the businesses that have been here long before me and I'll be funding the restoration of the water fountain."

Silence.

Then, "You're serious?"

He nods. "Completely."

Another beat of silence, then Thomas lets out a heavy breath and claps. Eva follows, and soon others join in. Another joins in and suddenly, the mood shifts. There's cautious optimism in the air.

Ben lets them have their moment, then says, "I don't expect you to trust me overnight. But I want to earn it."

I stare at him, my heart hammering, something unsteady curling in my chest.

\*\*\*

I wait as the last of the crowd disperses, watching Ben. He stands there, hands still in his pockets, eyes heavy with something I can't quite name. When the last person finally leaves, it's just the two of us, the rustling leaves and distant hum of the city our only company.

He turns to me, his expression gentler now. "I'm sorry I left early," he says softly. "There was some unfinished business I needed to handle."

He pauses, a flicker of something unreadable in his eyes—something darker, quieter. "Old ghosts, I guess."

I swallow hard, suddenly finding it difficult to speak.

"I meant what I said," he murmurs. "I know I've been a complete prick. I know I don't deserve an easy fix. But I need you to know that this—" he gestures around us, "—it was never about revenge. I was just a greedy bastard who thought I could bulldoze my way through everything and call it business."

I let out a shaky breath, my fingers curling into my sleeves.

His jaw tightens, and for the first time, I see it—the vulnerability he's trying so hard to mask. The hesitation in his eyes, like he's bracing for me to shut him down.

"I've spent years convincing myself I didn't need you, that I could move on, build something bigger, be someone bigger." His voice cracks slightly, but he pushes through. "But I was lying. To myself. To everyone. You were always there, even when you weren't. I know I've been a selfish bastard, but I swear, Lila, if there's even the smallest chance you could trust me again—I'll do whatever it takes."

My breath catches. "Ben..."

He sighs, rubbing the back of his neck, his shoulders dropping slightly. He looks down, shifting his weight from one foot to the other, and for a moment, I see it—the seventeen-year-old boy who once stood outside my house, nervous and hopeful, asking me out for the first time.

That same hesitation flickers in his eyes now. Just Ben, stripped bare, laying himself out before me.

"I've made a mess of everything, and I know that. But for the first time in a long time, I don't have some grand plan or calculated move. It's just me, standing here, hoping like hell you don't walk away."

My heart pounds so hard I swear he can hear it. The world around us seems to shrink, the distant hum of the city fading into nothing. This moment, everything feels surreal—like something out of a dream I've had too many times but never let myself believe in. My fingers tremble at my sides, my breath catching in my throat. I want to say something, to move, to reach for him—but I'm frozen, trapped between the past and the terrifying possibility of a future I never thought I could have again.

Ben exhales, the tension in his shoulders barely easing, like he's bracing himself for the worse. The wind stirs between us, carrying the scent of the trees and the faint murmur of voices in the distance. His fingers twitch at his sides, like he wants to reach for me, but doesn't know if he should. Finally, he speaks.

"I– I have to go back to London. Wrap up some projects, deal with the fallout of my grand declaration this morning. But I'll come back—if you'll have me."

He reaches for my hand, his fingers warm against mine. My pulse stutters as he presses something into my palm—a small envelope.

"Open it later," he says, his lips brushing my forehead in a feather-light kiss. "I'll be waiting."

*****

The cafe is dark except for the soft glow of fairy lights strung along the walls, casting a warm, golden hue over the empty space. The closed sign hangs on the door, but inside, it's just me and the girls—our private Books that Bang book club, which tonight was supposed to double as a celebration. Except I don't feel like celebrating.

I sit at the counter instead of our usual table, the envelope resting in front of me, my fingers tracing over the edges. The smell of coffee lingers, comforting yet grounding, making this all feel too real. My friends chat around me, sipping wine and laughing, but it doesn't take long before they realise I'm not chiming in.

"You look like someone hit you with a freight train," Olivia says, sliding into the seat across from me, eyeing me like

## LILA

I should be bouncing with excitement. "Shouldn't we be celebrating? The town's saved. Evil developer reformed. Cue the happy ending."

I let out a sigh, rubbing a hand over my face. "Because it's not that simple." They blink at me, confused. With my heart in my throat, I spill everything.

They listen. They let me speak and when it's all out, I drop my gaze to the table, my finger tracing invisible lines. I'm a tangled mess of feelings and I don't know what to do with any of it.

Sophie's eyebrows shoot up. "In here? Damn, Lila."

Olivia smacks her arm. "Focus."

Willow tilts her head. "Do you regret it?"

I shake my head instantly. "No. That's the problem. It wasn't just sex. It was... as if I found a part of me again and I want more—that terrifies me."

Olivia exhales. "Because if it's real, that means it could fall apart again."

I nod, my throat tight. "Exactly. I don't get happy endings, guys. I've watched people leave my whole life. My dad, Ben, nearly this whole damn town at one point. I've fought for everything I have and now I feel like I'm standing on the edge of a cliff. If I jump, I don't know if there's going to be anything to catch me."

Willow reaches across the table and grabs my hand, squeezing tight. "Lila, I need you to hear me," she says, her voice softer than I've ever heard it. "We may not have known each other our whole lives, but sometimes, it feels like I've known you forever. You, Olivia, Sophie—you're my family and family means sticking around, no matter what."

My chest tightens, the weight of her words pressing against

something raw inside me.

"You think you're alone in this, but you're not," she continues. "You'll always have us. Whether you jump or not, whether it works out with Ben or it doesn't, we're here and we're not going anywhere."

I blink rapidly, willing the tears not to fall. "Why do you guys always do this?" I mutter, attempting a weak laugh. "I came here to sulk, not get a therapy session."

Sophie grins. "Too bad. You're stuck with us."

Olivia nudges my arm. "You deserve love, Lila. The kind that doesn't leave. If there's even a chance Ben could be that for you, don't you think you owe it to yourself to find out?"

I stare at them, at the unwavering belief in their eyes, and something inside me shifts. With trembling fingers, I reach for the envelope. My breath stutters as I tear it open, my heart hammering against my ribs. The paper inside feels fragile, aged—like something kept safe for too long.

Then I see it.

The origami crane. My origami crane, the one I made for him all those years ago. The once-bright blue paper has faded to a muted, dusky shade, the edges worn soft with time. There's a tiny tear near the wing, barely noticeable, but I see it—just like I see the faint smudge of ink where I had once doodled a tiny star in the corner, now almost completely rubbed away.

A choked sob rips from my throat as the realisation crashes over me. He kept it. Through everything. Through time, through distance, through heartbreak. He held onto this tiny, delicate piece of us.

Tears spill down my cheeks, my hands shaking as I clutch it to my chest.

"Oh, Lila," Olivia whispers, her voice thick with emotion.

## LILA

She slides into the seat beside me and pulls me into a tight hug. Willow and Sophie follow, arms wrapping around me, anchoring me in a way I didn't know I needed.

"If that's not love," Olivia murmurs, brushing a tear from my cheek, "I don't know what is."

I let out a watery laugh, shaking my head. "I don't know what to do."

Willow squeezes my hand. "I think you know."

I glance down at the crane again, my vision blurred with tears. Maybe she's right. Maybe I've always known.

I think... It's time to stop running.

# 21

# Ben

It's been seven days since I left Nottingham. Seven days since I last saw Lila. Seven days of pretending I have my shit together when, in reality, I'm barely keeping my head above water.

I've thrown myself into work, kept my schedule packed, signed deals, sat through meetings, and handled everything I promised the residents—funds allocated, restoration projects initiated, investments restructured—but none of it has quieted the ache in my chest.

Because no matter how much I try to distract myself, I keep thinking about her.

I check my phone for the millionth time. No messages. No calls. I've wanted to call her every damn day since I left, but I told myself I wouldn't.

For once, I needed to give her space.

I barged back into her life, tore through it like a wrecking ball, made decisions for her, around her, about her. If I want to prove I've changed, this is where it starts and yet... every second apart is driving me fucking insane.

I rub my temples, exhaling sharply. My office overlooks

the London skyline, pristine glass panels reflecting the grey afternoon light. The contrast between here and Nottingham couldn't be starker. My world in London is controlled, predictable. Lila is none of those things. She's colour and warmth and life—and I miss her like hell.

As I pass Claire's desk, she steps into view, her tone brisk and efficient. "Your two o'clock's already here. They turned up early, so I had them wait in your office."

I pause, a flicker of annoyance tightening my jaw. "Early?"

"Fifteen minutes," she says with a nod, expression unreadable

I sigh, adjusting the cuffs of my suit. Fine. Let's get this over with. I straighten my spine, preparing for yet another meeting that will mean nothing in the grand scheme of things. Another deal, another contract, another distraction.

When I push the door open, I stop breathing.

Because sitting there, in my sterile, painfully modern office, is Lila.

She's perched on the edge of one of my sleek leather chairs, a stark contrast to the sharp lines and minimalist décor around her. She's wearing a dress—soft, flowy, a little vintage, a little shabby chic—something that doesn't belong in this cold, corporate space.

She looks like she's stepped out of a different world and into mine and fuck me, I've never seen anything more beautiful.

For a second, I can't move, can't speak, can't breathe.

Then she looks up, meeting my gaze with those big, soul-wrecking eyes, and my whole world tilts.

Lila blinks up at me, uncertain, hesitant, but here. She's here.

My grip tightens on the doorknob, grounding myself. I half expect her to disappear if I move too fast, like this is another cruel hallucination conjured by my sleep-deprived brain.

But she doesn't vanish. She just sits there, her fingers smoothing over the hem of her dress, as if she's just as overwhelmed as I am.

I don't take my eyes off her as I reach for the desk phone, pressing the button to call Claire.

"Yes, Mr Ashcroft?"

"Cancel the rest of my meetings." My voice is rough, uneven.

There's a beat of silence before she replies, amused. "Already done, sir."

I exhale sharply. Smart woman. Mental note: Give Claire a pay rise.

I set the receiver down, but I don't move closer. Not yet. Instead, I watch Lila, waiting for her to speak first, because I need to hear why she's here.

She finally stands, smoothing her hands down her dress, glancing around my office like she doesn't belong here. She doesn't. She's too soft, too vibrant, too real for this cold, lifeless space.

"I like your office," she says, though her voice lacks conviction.

I smirk, stepping toward her. "Liar."

She lets out a small huff of laughter. "Yeah. It's awful."

Just like that, the tension shatters.

I take another step, closing the space between us, my pulse pounding. She's here. She's in front of me and I can't go another second without knowing why.

"Lila." I exhale her name like a prayer. "Tell me why you're here."

She lifts her chin, meeting my gaze head-on. Brave. Always brave.

## BEN

Instead of answering, she reaches into the cotton bag slung over her shoulder and pulls something out. My brows furrow as she holds it up, and then I see it—the Mr & Mrs mug set.

The same one I sent her weeks ago. My chest tightens as she walks over to my desk, places the "Mr" mug on the polished surface, and picks up a Sharpie.

I watch in stunned silence as she uncaps it, leans over, and in bold, deliberate strokes, writes "On Trial" beneath the word Mr.

My lips twitch despite the pounding of my heart.

She turns back to me, arching a brow. "I take commitments very seriously, Ben."

I cross my arms, intrigued. "Do you?"

She nods, all mock-seriousness, adjusting the mug with deliberate precision. "You'll have to interview for the position."

I huff out a laugh, shaking my head as I take the cup from her. "An interview?"

She shrugs, biting back a smile. "These things require due diligence."

I glance at the mug, then back at her. "You know I like matcha, right?"

She smirks. "Good. Then you're already halfway qualified."

Something warm unfurls in my chest. This is Lila, my Lila—sharp, quick-witted, completely incapable of letting anything be easy.

I lean against my desk, admiring how fucking gorgeous she looks right now. "Alright, where's the interview happening?"

She strolls around my desk, eyeing my oversized executive chair like she owns the place, then lowers herself into it with a slow, deliberate movement. She crosses her legs, drumming her fingers on the armrest before tilting her head at me.

"Take a seat."

She gestures to the smaller chair across from her—the one reserved for interns, clients, people who answer to me.

My brow lifts.

Her lips curve, but there's no humour in it. "Do I look like I'm joking?"

I rake my teeth over my bottom lip, heat curling low in my stomach. Damn her. She's enjoying this.

I exhale sharply, playing along, but every fibre of my being is locked on her—the way she leans back like she belongs there, the way her dress slides higher as she crosses her legs again, the way her eyes dare me to push back.

I settle into the smaller chair, my knees brushing the desk, my pulse drumming in anticipation.

She tilts her head, studying me, her fingers tracing idly over the leather armrest.

"Much better."

Christ. I'm already half-hard, and we haven't even started.

"Your work history is... questionable. Given your prior offences, the board has some concerns."

I can't stop the grin that tugs at my lips. "Can I ask who's on this board, exactly?"

She steps closer, placing her hands on the armrests, caging me in. "Just me."

She pauses, tilting her head. "Although... I do have certain personal stakeholders who also have a vested interest in this decision."

I arch a brow. "Stakeholders?"

She nods solemnly. "Mmm. A very involved advisory panel. Passionate. Uncompromising. Should you fail to meet expectations, they will not hesitate to fire you."

## BEN

I huff out a laugh, already knowing exactly who she means.

I swallow hard as she slowly moves to straddle me, her soft floral dress brushing against my thighs as she settles into my lap.

Fuck.

She trails a finger down my chest, her eyes locked onto mine. "I take this process very seriously, Mr Ashcroft."

I exhale through my nose, my hands gripping her hips, holding her still even as every nerve in my body begs me to move. To take.

"Ms Ng." My voice is rough, strained. "What exactly are you assessing?"

She taps her chin, pretending to think. "Well, first—general competency. "Can you follow instructions? Take direction well?" Her lips twitch, but there's something deeper behind the teasing.

I clench my jaw, my grip tightening on her waist. "I think I can manage."

She hums, still toying with me, but then her expression softens. "But mostly... I need to know if you mean it. If this is real for you. If I can trust that you're not just here for the fight, for the challenge, for the thrill of getting what you couldn't have before."

Her fingers brush along my jaw, her voice quieter now. "I need to know if I'm safe with you."

My chest tightens—because this isn't just a question. It's everything.

I take her hand gently, guiding it to rest over my heart. "Lila," I murmur, holding her gaze, "you're the only thing I've ever been sure of."

A breath shudders past her lips before she kisses me—slow, searching, like she's trying to map every inch of what we lost, what we've found again. I groan into her mouth, my fingers tangling in her hair, tilting her head so I can take more, give more.

She tastes like home, like everything I've been missing and I don't want to come up for air.

Her hands frame my face, her thumbs brushing against my cheekbones, like she's trying to memorise me. "I missed you," she murmurs against my lips.

My grip tightens on her hips. "You have no idea."

I press my forehead to hers, my breaths ragged. "A week apart felt like a lifetime. I hated every second of it."

Her fingers slide down my chest, her eyes searching mine. "Then don't leave again."

Something breaks open inside me.

"I won't." I shake my head, swallowing hard. "I couldn't if I tried."

Her lips part, her breath hitching. "Ben..."

"I love you, Lila." The words tumble out, rough, raw, irrevocable. "I have for years, and I will for the rest of my life."

A soft, broken laugh escapes her, tears welling in her eyes, but she smiles—and then she launches herself at me.

Her lips crash against mine, her hands fisting my shirt, desperate, frantic, like she's been holding it in for years and can't bear another second of silence. I groan against her mouth, my grip on her hips tightening as she presses into me, claiming me just as much as I'm claiming her.

"I love you too," she breathes between kisses, her voice shaky, wrecked, perfect. She presses a hand to my chest, right over my pounding heart, like she needs to feel it, needs to know

## BEN

this is real.

I capture her mouth again, tilting my head, deepening the kiss, pouring every bit of longing, of lost time, of everything I can't put into words into her. She moans against my lips, her nails scraping down my chest as she shifts in my lap, her hips pressing down, driving me to the edge of insanity.

"Show me," she whispers, her voice thick with need, with urgency.

Something inside me snaps.

I groan, my hands gripping her thighs as I lift her slightly, my fingers bunching the fabric of her dress, pushing it up and out of my way. She's already bare beneath it, and fuck, I nearly lose my mind.

She gasps when I press my palm between her legs, finding her hot, wet, ready.

"Christ, Lila," I rasp, my control hanging by a thread.

She grinds against my hand, her breath stuttering. "No teasing, I need you. Now."

I don't hesitate. My fingers work at my belt, my trousers, shoving them down just enough, freeing myself, my cock aching to be inside her.

She rises slightly, guiding me to where we both need and then—she sinks down, taking me in one smooth, desperate motion.

A strangled groan rips from my throat.

"Fuck, Lila."

She cries out, her hands gripping my shoulders, her body stretching, adjusting, clenching around me like she was made for this. For me.

I thrust up into her, my grip on her hips bruising as she moves, riding me, taking me, owning me.

Her head tips back, her moans soft, breathless, perfect, and I can't stop kissing her—her throat, her jaw, her lips—wherever I can reach.

"Look at me," I demand, my voice rough, desperate.

She lifts her head, her gaze locking onto mine, blown wide with pleasure, with something deeper, something real.

"I love you," I rasp, pumping into her, meeting her every movement.

Her lips part, her breath catching. "I love you too."

I feel her fall apart around me, her body tightening, trembling, as she cries out my name, her fingers digging into my shoulders, her nails marking me, claiming me.

I lose it.

The sight of her—lips parted, eyes hazy, body quaking as she comes undone on top of me—it's too much, too fucking much.

I thrust up into her one last time, my grip on her hips bruising, my own release slamming into me like a tidal wave. A guttural groan rips from my throat as I spill into her, dragging her down onto me, holding her tight, as if letting go would mean losing her again.

She slumps forward, panting, shaking, her forehead resting against mine. Our breaths mix, our bodies still fused together, the air between us thick, heavy, electric.

I brush my lips over her cheek, her jaw, anywhere I can reach, still trying to catch my breath, still trying to comprehend that she's here.

Her fingers trace the back of my neck, her touch softer now, lingering, loving.

Neither of us speaks for a moment, too caught up in the aftershocks, the weight of what just happened, of what it means.

Then, in a whisper so soft I barely hear it, she breathes. "You got the job."

# 22

# Lila

**Several Months Later**

The sun is dipping low, casting long shadows over the nearly finished park. The new water fountain gleams in the evening light, benches freshly painted, fairy lights already strung between the trees, waiting to be switched on tomorrow.

There's just a few final things to do.

Right now, Ben is being bossed around like a rookie intern by my mother.

I spot him near the flower beds, looking deeply offended by a gardening trowel, his sleeves rolled up, expensive watch still on, as if he's trying to maintain some level of dignity while on his knees in the dirt. I bite back a laugh, walking over as Mum shakes her head at him. "Benjamin, you are murdering that poor lavender plant."

Ben sighs dramatically, wiping the back of his hand across his forehead like he's been working the fields for hours instead of planting a few flowers. "With all due respect, Mrs Ng," he says, voice painfully polite, "the plant is not dead. It's merely…

adjusting to my technique."

Mum huffs, shaking her head. "For a man who can handle billion-pound deals, you have the delicate touch of a wrecking ball."

Mum smacks his shoulder lightly with a gardening glove, muttering something in Cantonese that is not a compliment before turning to grab another plant.

I crouch beside Ben, smirking. "You know, if you just followed directions, she might go easier on you."

He levels me with a flat look. "Lila, I could buy an entire landscaping company and have them redo this entire park overnight. Instead, I am here, in the dirt, receiving a performance review from your mother." He exhales, running a hand through his slightly mussed hair. "If this isn't love, I don't know what is."

Damn it, my heart squeezes.

I brush my fingers over his, squeezing lightly. "You're doing great, babe."

He glances at the plant, then back at me, deadpan. "Liar."

I bite my lip to keep from laughing. "No, really. You've got that rugged, hardworking man aesthetic going on. Very sexy. Dirt-streaked forearms? Rolled-up sleeves? It's doing things for me."

He quirks a brow, clearly not buying it, but more than happy to play along. "Oh? So all it takes is a little manual labour and suddenly I'm your fantasy?"

I lean in slightly, my voice dropping just enough to make his eyes darken. "Mmm. Maybe. Though I usually prefer men who know what they're doing with their hands."

His grip on the trowel tightens, and I swear I see his jaw clench.

"Oh, sweetheart." He shifts, suddenly much closer than he

needs to be, his voice low, smooth, dangerous. "You and I both know my hands aren't the problem."

Heat flares low in my stomach, but before I can fire back, Mum calls from the other side of the herb garden. "Lila, stop distracting him," she says, exasperated. "That poor plant has suffered enough."

I smirk, still holding Ben's gaze. "Right. Wouldn't want to overwhelm him."

Ben exhales, rubbing a hand over his face like he's deeply regretting every life choice that led him to this moment. Then, without missing a beat, he mutters, "If your mother wasn't standing right there, I'd have you on this ground right now, dirt be damned."

Heat flashes through me, my smirk faltering for half a second before I regain my composure. I tilt my head, dragging my fingers slowly down his arm, my voice all sugar and sin. "Oh? Here I thought you hated manual labour."

His grip tightens on the trowel, his gaze dark, hungry. "There's one kind I happen to be very, very good at."

A flush creeps up my neck, but before I can reply, Mum clears her throat again—louder this time. "Benjamin. Less talking, more planting."

I bite back a laugh, stepping away and patting his shoulder with faux sympathy. "Better get to work, babe. Can't have my mum thinking you're all talk and no action."

His eyes flash with a promise. "Oh, sweetheart. When we get home, we'll see who's all talk."

\*\*\*\*

The park is alive with laughter, music, and the hum of conversation. The fairy lights glow softly against the evening sky, illuminating the newly restored fountain as water cascades elegantly into the basin. Everywhere I look, there's life.

Children race across the grass, weaving between groups of people, their excited shrieks blending with the soft melodies of the live band. Thomas's bakery has set up a stall, filling the air with the scent of warm bread and pastries, while Clara's salon is running a mini beauty booth, painting the little girls' nails with glittery polish that catches the light.

This place has never felt more alive.

Right in the middle of it? Ben.

He's deep in conversation with the mayor, his dark jeans hugging his frame just right, a crisp button-down with the sleeves rolled up to his forearms, the top two buttons undone. Relaxed. Effortless. He belongs here. His stance is relaxed, his smile genuine, and for the first time, he's not just an outsider looking in—he's part of this.

I watch as Maeve—who has become increasingly obsessed with bossing him around—marches up to him with a clipboard in hand.

"Benjamin," she says crisply, adjusting her dress up glasses. "Are you enjoying the event?"

Ben blinks, his expression shifting from mild amusement to wary curiosity. "Uh... yes?"

She nods, scanning her clipboard. "Good. Because I'm going to need you to help serve the desserts in precisely twenty minutes."

His brows lift, a slow smirk tugging at his lips. "I—what?"

Maeve doesn't even blink. "You helped save this park, didn't you? You're part of this community now, aren't you?"

I press a hand over my mouth to smother my laughter, watching as Ben visibly weighs his options.

Finally, he exhales, playing along, utterly charmed despite himself. "Fine. But if I do this, you promise to give me a ten-minute break afterward?"

Maeve taps her pen against the clipboard, considering. "Five."

Ben tilts his head, eyes narrowing in mock offence. "Seven."

She squints up at him, her tiny frame somehow managing to look intimidating. "Six."

Ben sighs, shaking his head, his lips twitching. "Deal."

Maeve nods approvingly, then immediately pivots, her mission far from over. She turns on her heel and zeroes in on Marcus, who has just taken a sip of his drink, completely unaware that he's about to be recruited.

Ten minutes later, Marcus comes back with Maeve, perched on Marcus's shoulders, looking like a queen surveying her kingdom.

Ben spots them at the same time as I do, raising a brow as Marcus trudges toward us, one arm bracing Maeve's leg while the other wipes sweat from his brow.

Marcus stops right in front of Ben and levels him with a look. "Your turn."

Ben blinks. "What?"

Maeve grins down from her throne, waving. "Benjamin, I request a shoulder ride!"

Ben coughs, shifting slightly. "I—uh—"

Marcus doesn't wait for an answer. He grips Maeve's waist, lifting her off his shoulders like she weighs nothing, and deposits her straight into Ben's arms.

Ben catches her on instinct, looking comically stunned as Maeve settles herself in like she's just upgraded to a better ride.

Marcus rolls his shoulders out, sighing in relief. "I like you,

Ashcroft, but if you try to give this one a corporate job in ten years, I will personally end you."

Ben huffs a laugh, adjusting Maeve slightly before glancing at Marcus. "Noted."

Marcus watches him for a beat, then extends his hand. Ben grips it, firm and steady. A silent truce. An understanding. A real welcome.

"I mean it, though. You did good here. The town's better for it."

Ben inclines his head. "Appreciate that."

Marcus smirks, shaking his head. "Though if you ever get tired of spreadsheets, I might have some real work for you."

Ben shrugs. "I'll pass. I hate manual labour."

Marcus chuckles, glancing at Maeve, who is now patting Ben's head like a pet. "Good luck with that one."

Ben sighs. "I'm already regretting this."

Maeve straightens up, gripping his shoulders like she's preparing for battle. "Away! Horsy!"

Before Ben can argue, Olivia appears, looking exasperated, shaking her head as she steps up beside Marcus. "I am so sorry."

Ben raises a brow. "For what, exactly?"

Olivia gestures vaguely at Maeve, who is now dramatically pointing into the distance like she's commanding an army. "She accidentally watched an episode of Judge Judy last week, and now she thinks she's a high-powered authority figure."

Marcus snorts. "Accidentally?"

Olivia rubs her temples. "I was watching it. She wandered in, got way too into it, and now she walks around saying things like, 'I will be making my ruling shortly' and 'You are in contempt!'"

Ben grins, completely charmed despite himself. He looks up

at Maeve. "So what's the verdict, your honour?"

Maeve nods seriously, tapping her chin. "Verdict is... you are a very slow horse. Move it."

Ben lets out a long-suffering sigh, adjusting his grip on her before jogging forward, making her shriek with laughter.

Marcus watches him go, shaking his head. "That poor bastard. He never stood a chance."

Olivia crosses her arms, smirking. "Nope. He's officially one of us now."

The night flows seamlessly, the celebration carrying on as champagne flutes are passed around. My mum gives a toast, people cheer, and the sound of clinking glasses fills the air.

I grab a flute. Willow does the same, and Olivia downs hers immediately.

But Sophie?

Sophie accepts hers, then pauses, glancing at it for just a second too long.

Before she can react, Marcus is already at her side with Maeve, taking the glass from her and replacing it with a fresh one from the bar.

Sophie narrows her eyes up at Marcus, but before Sophie can talk, Maeve claps her hands together, beaming. "Because Auntie Sophie can't drink alcohol anymore!"

The entire table goes still.

Sophie closes her eyes, exhales sharply. "Marcus."

Olivia gasps so hard I think she might inhale her entire drink. Willow's jaw drops.

"You're PREGNANT?!" Willow practically screeches, grabbing Sophie's arm like she's about to shake the truth out of her.

Sophie groans, rubbing her temples. "Well. There goes my

plan of telling you all like normal people."

"I KNEW it!" Olivia practically bounces on the spot. "I had a feeling! Last week you turned down sushi—SUSHI, Sophie. I should have called it then!"

I give her a hug. "How far along are you?"

Sophie blushes. "Eleven weeks."

Sophie shoots Marcus a glare. "This is your fault."

Marcus arches a brow, completely unbothered. "Of course, it's my fault. I did, after all, have unprotected sex with you. I feel like that's where it all started."

Sophie gapes at him. "Marcus!"

Marcus smirks, looping an arm around her waist and pulling her against him. "What? Actions have consequences, baby mama."

Willow snorts into her champagne. "Wow. Romance is truly alive and well."

We all dissolve into laughter, and I take a step back, watching them, watching this moment, this night.

Everything around me feels perfect.

My mum steps up beside me, watching the chaos unfold with a small smile. She pulls me aside, her gaze lingering on Ben, who's still carrying Maeve while making casual conversation with the mayor.

Mum sighs, nudging me gently. "He fits here, you know."

I glance over at Ben again—who's already looking at me, like he knew I'd turn to find him.

"Yeah," I whisper. "He does."

She nods slowly, her expression softening. "He makes you happy."

"He does," I say quietly, warmth swelling in my chest.

Mum smiles, her hand squeezing my arm. "Good. That's all

that matters."

She hesitates for a beat, then adds, "You know… I was worried about leaving. About the cafe. About you."

I turn to her, but she's already watching Ben again, her voice quieter now. "You've got Jess taking on more shifts, the cafe's thriving… you've really built something special here. But part of me still feels guilty about going."

I smile softly, nudging her. "Mum, you don't need to worry about me. I'll be fine. Honestly, everything's running smoothly, and you've earned this. Go. Enjoy it. You've spent your whole life looking after everyone else—it's your turn now."

She hesitates, eyes glistening just a little. "It's just… a round-the-world cruise. Me and the girls. I still can't believe he did that."

I laugh, my chest tightening with emotion. "Of course he did. You deserve it."

She nods, her expression full of warmth and pride. "So do you."

Maeve's giggle cuts through the air as Ben lifts her higher, his deep chuckle following right behind.

Just like that, I know.

# 23

## Epilogue - Ben

I follow the sound, leaning casually in the doorway of her flat. She's perched on the counter, tea in one hand, video call propped up in front of her, talking to Olivia—who currently looks like she's been personally victimised by the sun.

"Olivia, are you okay? You look like you've just stepped out of a sauna," Lila says, half-laughing as Olivia aggressively fans herself with a laminated brochure.

"It's not a sauna," Olivia groans. "It's *Texas*. There is no air. There is only heat and dust and the overwhelming stench of livestock."

"You said it was a boutique wellness retreat," Lila teases.

"I WAS LIED TO," Olivia practically shrieks, sweat-slicked hair sticking to her forehead. "There's a goat outside my window. A goat, Lila."

I chuckle under my breath, arms folded. Olivia's trip was meant to be soul-searching. So far, it's looking more like accidental farm work.

Olivia adjusts the camera and accidentally pans across the ranch behind her.

Lila's eyes narrow, her head tilting slightly. "Wait... who is *that*?"

The camera lingers for a split second on a man walking across the courtyard—tall, broad shoulders, cowboy hat low over his eyes, sleeves rolled up over solid forearms that glint in the sun. He looks like he stepped off a damn romance novel cover.

Before I can blink, Olivia yanks the phone back toward her face. "No one!"

Lila's grin widens instantly. "That was *not* no one. That was someone. And holy hell, he's hot."

My brows lift.

Hot?

I step further into the kitchen, reaching around her to steal her tea. "I'm sorry—*hot*?"

Lila smirks over her shoulder at me. "Relax, caveman."

"That little mouth's gonna get you into trouble, sweetheart," I murmur low in her ear.

Olivia makes a gagging sound from the phone speaker. "Urgh! Seriously, I did not sign up for this audio erotica."

Lila bursts out laughing, swatting at me while I just grin and kiss the top of her head. "He's the owner," Olivia mutters. "Colt Lawson. The ranch's been in his family for generations or some sentimental crap. Why he ever thought hospitality was his calling is beyond me—he's got the people skills of a cactus."

Lila smirks. "If it's that bad, why don't you go to another hotel?"

There's a pause.

Then Olivia coughs. "His mum makes the best food I've ever tasted."

Lila arches a brow. "Ah. So you're suffering in silence for the lasagna."

"I'm suffering for her peach cobbler, actually," Olivia huffs. "Woman's a culinary saint. It's a damn emotional hostage situation. I'd sleep in a goat pen if it meant getting another plate of her cornbread."

Lila's eyes sparkle with mischief. "Nothing to do with the hot, brooding cowboy riding past your window every morning?"

"Goodbye!" Olivia hangs up dramatically, and Lila's still giggling as she sets her phone aside. The laughter lingers for a moment... then fades, softening into something quieter, gentler. She glances over at me, her smile dimming slightly, not in sadness—but in understanding. Her eyes meet mine, warm and steady.

"You ready?" she asks softly.

I pause.

The question isn't about dinner. Or bed. Or anything light.

For a moment, something catches in my chest—tight and unfamiliar.

But then I nod.

Not big. Not bold. Just enough.

"Yeah," I say quietly. "I think I am."

She steps closer, slipping her hand into mine.

*****

The scent of burning incense drifts through the crisp morning air, curling in soft, lazy ribbons. The cemetery is quiet, save for the occasional rustle of leaves, the distant murmur of families speaking in hushed voices, the rhythmic brush of a broom against stone.

I kneel beside Lila, my fingers tight around the bundle of incense sticks I haven't yet lit. I exhale slowly, glancing at her out of the corner of my eye. She's calm, practiced, focused, arranging the offerings with careful hands.

I'm out of my element. Completely.

Qingming Festival. Tomb-Sweeping Day. A tradition that's not mine, not something I grew up with. But Lila had explained it to me—a day for honouring the dead, for tending graves, for remembering.

Today, we're here for my mother.

I swallow, staring at the headstone in front of me. Katherine Ashcroft etched into the stone feels both familiar and foreign, like I've spent years trying not to look at it too closely.

I set down the bouquet of sweet peas I brought, but I feel so out of place.

Lila notices, she always does.

She doesn't say anything at first, just reaches over and takes the incense from my hands, her fingers brushing over mine. She lights them, then passes them back to me, her eyes soft, knowing.

"You don't have to say anything out loud" she murmurs, her voice soft, steady. "Just... say whatever you need to in here." She presses a gentle hand over my chest, right above my heart.

I hesitate. What the hell do I even say?

*I'm sorry, I should have been there. I should have done better.*

The words stick in my throat, heavy, tangled.

So I do the only thing I can—I bow my head and let the silence speak for me. The incense smoke curls upward, disappearing into the sky, carrying whatever unspoken words I can't seem to say aloud.

I exhale slowly, gripping the incense just a little tighter.

## EPILOGUE - BEN

"Mum. I lost everything after you, but somehow... I found her."

Lila stills beside me, her fingers grazing my knee.

"Thank you for helping me find my way back. I'm sorry it took so long."

My chest tightens, but for the first time in a long time, it doesn't feel suffocating—it feels right.

I swallow hard, my gaze fixed on the name carved into stone. "I love her."

I set the incense in its holder, watching the embers flicker before I let Lila pull me up, her fingers twining with mine. She doesn't say anything.

She just leans into me, presses her forehead against my shoulder and holds on.

For the first time in years, I don't feel like I'm walking away from my past.

I feel like I'm bringing it with me.

\*\*\*\*\*\*

I unlock the door and step inside, holding it open with a grin. "After you."

Lila raises a brow, but she walks in ahead of me, her eyes sweeping over the space we've spent months creating together—our home. A blend of her vision and my hands. She might have a knack for picking paint swatches and knowing exactly which lights make a room feel like a warm hug, but it was my tools, my sweat, my late nights that turned those sketches into reality.

I could've paid someone to do it—hell, I've got teams who've built half my damn empire. But this? This needed to be me. Every beam, every floorboard, every inch of this place had to come from my hands. Because this isn't just another project. It's *ours*.

She moves through the open-plan living room, her fingers brushing over the rich textures, her gaze flicking over the archway we argued about for weeks—and that she was, of course, completely right about. Her smile is soft, proud. She pauses near the window seat she designed, the one I built with reclaimed timber, just the way she wanted.

"You did good," she murmurs, turning to me.

I shrug, trying for nonchalance. "You're the boss, sweetheart. I just follow orders."

She gives me a look that says she knows damn well how many late nights I spent making her vision come to life. "And don't think I didn't notice you sneak in those brass fixtures I said were too expensive."

I smirk. "Couldn't resist. You've got good taste."

She shakes her head, laughing softly. "It's perfect."

But I'm not done. I bend, wrapping an arm under her legs, lifting her clean off the floor.

A startled laugh bursts from her lips. "Ben!"

I grin, carrying her deeper into the house. "Tradition, sweetheart."

She shakes her head, laughing, but doesn't let go.

I don't put her down until we reach the bedroom.

The moment I push open the door, she sucks in a breath.

Candles flicker everywhere—soft, golden light dancing over the room.

The bed is done up with crisp sheets, a deep navy throw, and a ridiculous amount of pillows that I will not be taking responsibility for.

Lila's face lights up. "You brought my book?"

I smirk. "Thought I'd brush up on what the girls in *Books That Bang* are into lately. Regency smut seems to be trending."

She laughs softly, biting her lip in that way that always ruins me. "And? What did you learn, Mr. Ashcroft?"

I close the space between us, my fingers trailing down her arms, over her waist, slow, deliberate. "Apparently, libraries are one of the most popular places to fuck." Her breath hitches, but she doesn't miss a beat. "Is that so?" She tilts her head towards me. "Wanna see what the hype is about?"

I groan, pressing my forehead to hers, smirking despite the burn low in my gut. "Sweetheart, as much as I'd love to bend you over a bookshelf right now..." I brush my lips over hers, slow and hot. "I want the first time in our home to be you, flat on that brand-new bed, screaming my name."

She shivers, her fingers curling into my shirt.

"Let me fuck you properly," I rasp, voice thick. "Slow. Deep. The way you deserve. Let me christen our goddamn bed."

I slide my hands to her hips, pulling her flush against me, my mouth brushing hers. "And then tomorrow—every room, every surface. Kitchen counter, window seat, library desk..." I bite her bottom lip gently, tugging it between my teeth before letting it go. "I'll make you come against every wall in this house, until you can't walk past a single spot without remembering what it felt like to fall apart underneath me."

Her breath catches, her lashes fluttering. "That's a lot of surfaces," she whispers, teasing.

I grin, dark and wicked. "Then you better start stretching, sweetheart."

And then I kiss her—deep, slow, consuming—like I'm already halfway there.

Because I am.


I take my time.

Tonight isn't about rushing—it's about knowing. About learning every inch of her, every sound she makes, every way she likes to be touched.

I start with the buttons of her dress, my fingers slow and deliberate, slipping them free one by one. The fabric loosens, parts, revealing more of her, inch by inch.

I brush my knuckles down her bare shoulder, watching as goosebumps rise in my wake.

She shifts under me, already restless, but I don't let her rush this.

I drag my mouth along her jaw, my voice low, steady. "Slow down, sweetheart." My lips trail lower, grazing the delicate skin of her collarbone. "Want to take my time with you."

Her hands tighten on my shoulders, her fingers curling into my shirt like she's considering tearing it off.

I move lower, my mouth following the path of my hands, my tongue flicking over the soft dip between her ribs, the sensitive spot just beneath her navel.

Her breath stutters, her hips shifting up, searching.

I grin against her skin, pressing a kiss right over her fluttering stomach.

"Something you like, baby?"

She glares down at me, her pupils blown wide, her chest rising and falling unevenly.

"If you stop now, I will smother you with that stupid book."

I laugh, nipping at her hip. "Noted."

## EPILOGUE - BEN

But I don't stop.

I explore.

I memorise.

I find out that she loves it when I suck on the inside of her thigh, just enough to leave a mark—but she loves it even more when I drag my teeth there first.

That when I brush my lips just behind her knee, she shivers, gripping the sheets like she's barely holding on.

That if I tease her too much, she'll yank me up by my hair and tell me to quit acting like a damn tease and do something about it.

I do exactly that.

She's so responsive, her moans turning into soft, breathy curses, then my name, then just wordless sounds that go straight to my dick.

I drag my mouth back up her body, relishing every damn second of it.

Her fingers slide into my hair, tugging hard.

"Ben."

My name isn't a plea. It's a command.

Her nails dig into my shoulders. "More."

Who the hell am I to deny her?

I finally slide into her, slow and deep, her legs wrapped around my hips and her eyes locked on mine, it's not just sex anymore.

It's everything.

The years we lost. The pain. The fight. The love that never really died.

I thrust deeper, holding her hips steady, watching the way she unravels under me, like I'm rewriting every story she's ever read—every fantasy she's ever had.

And I think of a future.

Of filling this house with laughter.

Of her curled on the couch, reading, her belly round with our child.

Of tiny feet padding across the floor, bedtime stories whispered under blankets, a life so full it spills out of the walls we built together.

Lila clings to me, her nails biting into my shoulders, her breath catching with every movement.

"Don't stop," she gasps, eyes wide, wild, desperate.

"Never," I promise, my voice rough as I drive into her again and again, until we're both shuddering, panting, tangled in sheets and sweat and love.

She falls apart beneath me—gasping my name, body arching like it's too much—I follow her over the edge, spilling into her with a groan so guttural it feels like it's been building for years.

We collapse in a tangle of limbs and heartbeats, our bodies still tangled like neither of us wants to let go. I roll us onto our sides, pulling her against me, our legs tangled, my hand smoothing up and down her spine.

She lets out a sleepy sigh, her fingers trailing along my chest.

My chest tightens, but in the best way. Like something inside me finally, finally slots into place.

So I hold her tighter, anchoring her to me, burying my face in her hair and letting the peace settle deep in my bones.

Because I know now—I'm not just home.

I'm hers.

Always.

# 24

# Thank you!

I'm so grateful you spent your time with *Spring* and joined Lila and Ben's journey. It truly means the world to me and I hope their story brought you as much joy as it did for me to write (the longer days are finally here!)

**As a new author, every review and recommendation means everything**. If you enjoyed the book, I'd be incredibly grateful if you could leave a review or share it with a friend. Word of mouth helps readers discover my books and keeps me inspired to bring more characters to life!

**Want more?** Sophie's story kicked off in *Winter Vows*, so if you haven't met her and Marcus yet, head back and start the series—*Winter Vows* is out now!

Next up? *Summer Burn* is bringing the heat with Olivia, and trust me, she's about to get **hot and bothered** in ways she never expected. Want a sneak peek? Join my newsletter for exclusive content, updates, and all things *A Year of Desire*.

Until next time, stay warm—and I'll see you in *Summer*!

**Ursula**

xxx

## About the Author

Hi! I'm a UK-based author from the Midlands who loves reading and writing steamy romance novels filled with instalove, suspense, action, and plenty of spice. Growing up, I was discouraged to follow my love of arts to follow a more traditional career path, but now, as a parent to two young children, I've decided it's time to pursue my passion and show them the importance of chasing their dreams.

When I'm not writing, you'll find me having a brew, indulging in egg custards, or juggling a day job and parenting. Just don't tell my other half about my ever-growing craft cupboard!

If you'd like to follow my journey and stay up to date with my latest releases, click the Newsletter link below. I promise to value your time and privacy—no spam, just heartfelt updates.

Thank you for stopping by and supporting me in this exciting chapter of my life!

**You can connect with me on:**

🌐 https://www.ursulachang.com

**Subscribe to my newsletter:**

✉ https://subscribepage.io/sfS8Wj

# Also by Ursula Chang

From contemporary sparks to military heat, I love crafting fast, steamy reads packed with tension, passion, and irresistible chemistry. At the heart of every story are strong, determined women and the alpha men who can't resist them!

**Winter Vow**

*One Night. No Regrets—right?*

Sophie's sworn off men after a brutal betrayal—until one unforgettable night with Marcus Kingsley throws her plans into chaos. He's powerful, irresistible, and impossible to forget. But she's built walls for a reason, and Marcus isn't the kind to walk away.

Will she risk her heart for a love that feels too good to be true? Or convince herself that happy endings are just fiction?

**The first book in *A Year of Desire*—a sizzling new series full of passion, heart, and unexpected romance.**

**Download now and start the year with desire!**

**Spectre**

🔥 *She's running for her life. He's the masked ghost who won't let her fall.* 🔥

Dr. Eliza Harrington never expected her groundbreaking medical research to paint a target on her back.

With deadly forces closing in, her only protection is Spectre, an elite SAS operative who refuses to reveal his face. A ghost in the shadows, a man without a name – yet there's something about him she can't quite shake.

When an unexpected blizzard traps them in a remote cabin, the tension between them ignites into something just as dangerous as the threat hunting them.

**Onyx**

Emma rebuilt her life—guarded, untouchable, and done with men. But when her violent ex resurfaces, she's forced to turn to the last man she ever wanted to see again.

Onyx doesn't do second chances.

The gruff military operative swore he was done with Emma after rescuing her once in Romania. She's stubborn, infuriating—and impossible to forget. But protecting her means staying close. Too close.

She's in danger—but it's her heart that's truly at risk.